Martin Hamilton

Berkley's Bastards Book 3

KATHI S. BARTON

World Castle Publishing, LLC
Pensacola, Florida
Copyright © Kathi S. Barton 2022
Hardback ISBN: 9798361851300
Paperback ISBN: 9781958336830
eBook ISBN: 9781958336847
First Edition World Castle Publishing, LLC, November 7, 2022
http://www.worldcastlepublishing.com

Licensing Notes

Cover: Karen Fuller
Editor: Karen Fuller

Prologue

Martin put his hands under his legs. Trying to maintain a distance wasn't going to work, he realized when the kids came and stood in front of him. He'd been just about ready to go out on the deck—a little at a time, his therapist told him—but they started coming in. The little girl, he didn't know their names, just then got up on the couch with him and leaned close and laid her head on his shoulder. Martin was ready to leap up and run when she spoke to the other children.

"You remember that kid that was jumpy all the time?" They nodded, though he doubted the youngest had any idea what she was talking about. "You remember that they had to take him away one night?

On account'a him screaming all night?"

"Yeah, he wasn't right in the head." The little girl told the speaker to hush and to behave. "I didn't mean it in a bad way, Carol, but he was messed up in the head on account'a the drugs that his mom and dad gave him. Did someone give this man drugs?"

"No, they didn't. I'm not good around people." The little boy told him they were kids, not people. "Why would you think that makes any difference? I mean, you're still a person, right?"

"I guess so. But we won't ever hurt you none." Martin said he wasn't worried about them hurting him rather than the other way around. "You won't hurt us either, Mr. Hamilton. You're hurting in a place that needs to be fixed. Am I right?"

"Something like that. I was working one day and had a nervous breakdown. I couldn't take it any longer and decided to end my life." He'd not even told Caleb that when he'd asked him about his health. When the little girl pulled his hand out from under his leg, Martin let them see the scars there. She ran her little finger over the fresh scar, and Martin could feel some kind of kid magic coming from her. "I let my job nearly kill me. I should have paid attention to my mind and body, but I thought I was above all that. I thought it would just go away. But all it did was make me sicker and sicker."

The kids sat on the floor except for the little girl. Martin didn't know why he was able to talk to these children. He'd already told them more than he had anyone before. By degrees, he felt his body begin to relax, his mind clear of the need to take flight.

"My mom did that. Cut up herself in the bathtub one day while I was at school." Martin told the little boy he was sorry for his loss. "My name is Shawn. I was seeing a doctor after my mom died, and I found her lying there. Until my dad thought I was too much of a burden for him. He got himself a new wife, too, who didn't want me around. But my mom, she was good to me. Made me a nice cake for my birthday. My doctor told my dad I was way more depressed than he was and that I needed to keep seeing someone about it. These kids here, they helped me."

"My mom is gone too. Cancer." The kids all told him they were sorry. "Thank you for that. I'm wondering if that had a little to do with my breakdown."

"Yeah, everything does." The little girl next to him told him her name was Maddy. "Mine and Mikey's mom sold us off to the home we was at. Yasmine and Joey are going to adopt us all if there isn't anyone looking for the others. But Yasmine is my aunt on account'a her being our mom's sister. She's dead too, our mom, though I don't know nothing about her."

He'd known that too, of course, but hearing the accounting of it was...Martin didn't know, but he thought it was charming in a way. Less harsh than thinking about what he'd been told about Jasmine Dennis.

It wasn't long before they had him adjusting his seating, so he had two kids on either side of him. George was in his lap snoozing, and the other four were talking around him. Martin thought this was the best he'd felt in a good long time. Just them talking around him and not screaming and yelling at people.

He looked up when he heard someone whisper his name. It was Yasmine. Apparently, at some point, the kids had wandered off, and he'd been snoozing himself.

"Are you all right?" He told her he'd only just

been thinking. "I've been feeling the same sort of special magic they can give off. Even George has his own type of magic."

He watched her move to the other couch. She sat in the middle, directly across from him. Laughing just a little, she smiled and asked him if she'd done something stupid again.

"I doubt anyone would think anything you did was stupid, Yasmine. You're much too beautiful for that. I was just admiring how you get around in the house. And when you sat across from me, I thought for sure that I'd been fibbed to about your blindness." She thanked him for not calling her a cripple or handicapped. "I'm assuming from what I heard about your sister, that's who called you that."

"Yes, it was her. A lot of other people too, but my sister knew better. I only told her several times a day." She didn't elaborate, so he didn't pry. "You seem really relaxed right now. So I don't want to tense you up by asking the wrong questions. I'm assuming you believe that you're related to my husband and Caleb now. What are your plans if you have thought them through?"

"I've not. Not really. I have a home back in Tennessee. There are a great many memories there. While here, believe it or not, I've realized that they weren't all good ones either. My mom was a great person, but she was bitter too. Not just for having to raise me without help, but about everything. She was unhappy a great deal of the time. But I loved her." Yasmine told him that, of course, he did. "Not that she made it easy for me. Mom showed me how to live on my own. How to deal with overdue collection calls and mail. Just trash them until it was going to be shut off or taken away. Food from the kitchen was hit or miss. Mostly the missing part. But she did love me too. And told me that every day."

"I plan to do that with the others too. Tell them how much I love them. How proud I am about something they've done. I've never been a mom before and have very little to go by as a role model. I'm going to wing it, as I've heard Ed say on occasion." He laughed, another thing he'd missed doing since he'd been stressed. "What is it you want to do with your life now that you're here? The world is open for you. I've only just discovered, now that there is no pressure on me to work, I enjoy my job a good deal more."

"I used to be a stockbroker. I never really liked it, not even at the beginning. It paid well, and I was good at it. If push came to shove, I'd rather live on the streets than to have to go back to something like that." He thought about her question and what she'd said about her own job. "I'd like something like that. Something I could do and just be able to enjoy. One of the things I used to do was grow plants. Just little things like tomatoes and lettuce. It supplemented our food at home, and I could spend hours out in the sunshine. I even got to where I was growing little things in the house."

"I have plants in my office. When I'm needing something to bring me out of my thoughts, I just need to reach over and touch them. Joey got me a couple of herbs, too, that I can smell. It's lovely. Why don't you do that for a living?" He asked her what she meant. "I'm fairly certain there is a need for a greenhouse around here. I know there used to be one. If I were to ask, I'm betting Caleb might even own the building."

"I don't know that I'm ready to embark on something like that." She stood up, and he did as well.

"I didn't mean to offend you if I did."

"You didn't. I just need to see to dinner." She started for the doorway, again looking like a person with sight, and turned back to him at the last moment. "Four days ago, I didn't know I had a niece *and* a nephew. Four days ago, I didn't have any children to speak of. Four days ago, I made a decision that would change the course of my life and those of the five kids that I now have. I had no experience with children. I knew nothing of how to make sure they were fed well. Being blind didn't even come into the picture until we were all here. Was it a great deal? Hell yeah. Was I overwhelmed? Yes, right up until one of them took my hand into theirs. Would I do it again? Without hesitation. You should think more along the lines of how things will affect you in the long run rather than thinking about how they're going to make you feel right at this moment. Dinner will be in about ten minutes, Martin."

After she left him, Martin thought about what she had said and burst out laughing. She had just scolded him in a way that he was sure she didn't realize. Standing up, he decided he was going to find the children and hang out with the rest of the family. And as of the moment Yasmine left him, he thought he was a part of a wonderful family.

~*~

"I'm not sure what you want from me, Mr. Billows, but I'm not even in the state right now. I asked for and got approved to have this weekend off. I have to settle my brother's estate." Mr. Billows told her she had one hour before she was to report to work. "Not possible. As I have said to you numerous times now, I'm not going to be able to come in. For a great many reasons, but not being in the state should be enough to tell you I'm not going to make it."

"Gracie, I'm sick of dealing with your shit all the time. You had better be in here at the beginning of this shift, or you should start looking for another job. Employees like you are a dime a dozen." She let out a long breath. He couldn't just replace her, and she knew it. "What do you have to say to that?"

"What do you think?" He told her she was a smart girl for doing what he demanded. "No, you got it wrong. I'm not going to be coming in tonight or any other night. I'll be contacting the owner tomorrow as well. If you're really that short-staffed, Mr. Billows, you should wait tables yourself. I'm finished."

It felt good to hang up on the man in mid-sentence. Before she could allow her doubts to settle in with her, she called the owner. Since she knew he'd be home today, it didn't bother her to call him at home. He had given her the number.

"Mr. Anderson, my name is Gracie Jefferies. I work at your restaurant called Devonshire. Mr. Billows just made it, so I've had to quit the restaurant, and I wanted to give you my side before he painted me as a bad person. I might need a reference from you or something. I doubt he'll do anything but slander my name four ways from Sunday." Mr. Anderson laughed, and she had to smile. He laughed like he didn't care one bit. "Yes, well, on my side, it's not all that funny. I explained to him that I had to settle my brother's estate for the bloodsucking attorneys. I haven't any idea why it has to be settled right this minute. As far as I can see, he didn't have a pot to piss in, much less the fancy name they're calling the estate. And I had asked for and was approved for the next four days off. I should be getting paid for it, as I've never had a day off in over sixteen months. I had to work the day we buried my brother." Gracie realized she was babbling and told the man what had happened.

"Gracie, did he ever allow you to train him on the closing procedures of the place? Or, for that matter, how to make out a schedule? Work that he should have been doing and wasn't?"

"I couldn't even try and show him how to rotate stock in the big fridge. He said whatever came out of the storage place would be used before its date, and I was to just leave it alone." He asked her if she'd done that. "No. Of course not. I know better than that. But I did ask for the time off, sir. I have the approval slip he signed the day I turned it in."

"I have no doubt that you have. And please accept my condolences on your brother's passing. I didn't know." She said he'd been sick for a long time. "Still, it is tragic. Let me know what attorney's office you're working with, and I'll find out what all the rush is about. That way, you can focus on what you're there to do. Where are you, anyway?"

"Ohio. A little town that no one has heard much about called Trinway." He laughed again. Gracie was beginning to think the man was off his rocker or something. Finding everything funny wasn't sane. "Anyway, you don't have to do that. I'll go there and take care of whatever they need, then clean out his house. I have to put it on the market as well right away, as he had built up medical bills more than the fund he was drawing on could cover. I have no idea why I'm telling you this."

"It sounds to me like you needed to vent, and I was the perfect person to do it to. But I know Trinway, Gracie. It's not far from Dresden, where I'm currently living. With my wife and brothers. I can get things taken care of for you right now." Again, she told him he didn't have to do that. "I don't. But I think you've done me a large favor by quitting your job today and finding out what Mr. Billows can do without you there running things for him. He's going to be in deep shit when the doors open, I think. Can you stay at your brother's place? Or do you need accommodations? I can do that for you if you wish."

"No, I can stay at my—what the hell is wrong with you?" He laughed again, and she felt her temper fall over her mouth. "You've done nothing but be nice to me since you went to the restaurant where I worked. Now you're being nice about my brother dying, getting me an attorney, and finding me digs to stay in. No one in their right mind is that nice."

"My wife would agree with you. But my mom taught me to help those that needed a hand up. She made it her life's work to do that. As for helping you in particular, you've been very nice to me in calling me and telling me the restaurant might be closed down tonight. Because as much as I'd like for the man to fail, he'll take my place with him. But only for tonight." She asked him if he could afford that. "I can. Even if I couldn't, it's a better way of him getting terminated than me calling him and doing it on— Ah. There he is now. Calling, no doubt, to tell me what a horrid person you are and that I should be grateful he's fired you."

"He didn't fire me. I'm sure it would have come to that, but Mr. Billows gave me an ultimatum that I couldn't work with. So I quit."

He asked her to hold on if she could. Telling him she could, Gracie watched the people playing in their yards while she waited.

Charlie had been ill since he was a child. He had

fallen out of a tree at the daycare center where the two of them had been taken while their parents worked. Charlie had been about four, not that she ever believed he'd been climbing a tree in the first place, but he had hit his head. Hard enough, her parents had been told that it cracked his skull. Since they'd had no insurance that would cover something like that kind of major surgery for a clumsy kid—they'd not even offered it to them—they'd not been able to afford for him to have whatever would be necessary for him to live.

To this day, she believed that one of the adults working at the daycare center had hurt him. The government not only provided her family with a food card, but they had paid for daycare so they'd not be a total burden on society. The insurance was all right—it covered a lot—but not nearly what they needed at that time.

Charlie could live alone only with someone coming in once a day to check on him. He could function well enough to work at a menial job, so long as it was repetitive and wasn't something that had to be done in a timeframe. He could do it; Charlie would work at a job all day and night, but once he was off the task for more than a few minutes, he'd have to be trained all over.

When Mr. Anderson came back on the phone, he asked her if he could message her something to her phone. Telling him that was fine, she wasn't sure what he'd have to say to her in a message that he couldn't say while they were speaking. Then he explained.

"That's the name of the attorney that is going to meet you at Bickerton and Bickerton in the morning. Arthur is a good attorney and a good friend. He said you were to dress casually, not dressed up. I'm not entirely sure why, but that's what he told me to tell you. Also, would you mind letting him make a copy of your permission slip from Billows? He's claiming you are fabricating all of this." She said she wasn't a liar. "I know that. All right. He's going to pick you up in the morning. I've already given him the address where you're staying."

"And just how did you come by that information?" His laughter again made her want to smack him. "Look, Mr. Anderson, I no longer work for you, so why the hell are you doing this? For a sense of enjoyment on my part? I won't think it's funny if I have to find my own way to the office in the morning and find out that being late or some shit is forfeiting whatever little bit my brother had to them. I think they're crooks, but I don't know a great deal about bloodsuckers."

"I have the best bloodsuckers in the world working for me. If I didn't, I'd not be as wealthy as I am." She told him to fuck off. "Thank you for that. It's refreshing to hear someone that isn't the least bit impressed by me or my money. I'll see you in the morning, Gracie. Good luck tomorrow."

After ringing off with him, she sat there long enough to look Mr. Anderson up. Whistling about what the news articles said about his money, she put her phone away. Not that she felt any better about him helping her, but she knew now that he could well afford it.

Starting her rental up, she made her way to her brother's home. When their parents had died, there had been a little money put away. They'd also been able to afford to purchase them a little house that just happened to be in a place that was developing into a nice neighborhood. She'd been able to sell it for about ten times more than her parents had paid for it and buy the house that Charlie was living in. Having it outfitted for his needs took all the rest of the money.

Going into the house, it occurred to her that this would be the last time she was here before selling it off. That her brother, her hero, wasn't going to come around the corner and tell her to wipe her feet. Wiping at her tears, she turned her phone off when Mr. Billows's name came up.

There wasn't much in the place that she'd have to deal with. Clothing, of course. His books too. Charlie loved to read when he needed to unwind. She did as well. The furniture had to be taken care of. Mostly she thought she'd give it away or donate it. Gracie thought someone could use it.

Getting her things out of the car, she pulled out the large trash bags she'd had at home and started in his bedroom. It took her nearly two hours to bag up items that still smelled like Charlie.

At about six, someone knocked on the door. While she wasn't sure if the neighbors knew her brother all that well, she went to check to see who was there. Opening the door, knowing that small towns weren't as safe as everyone assumed they were, she left the chain on the door.

"Ms. Jefferies, my name is Arthur Fowler. Mr. Anderson, Caleb, sent me here to bring you some dinner, and I'd like to go over any information you might be able to help me with concerning your brother's health and his estate." She opened the door wider and asked to see his identification. "Yes, of course. I should have thought of that."

After checking it out, she allowed him in the house. Before she could close the door behind him, he waved for the people she'd not seen to come into the house as well. They were delivery people. The smells coming from the many bags they had made her realize she had not just skipped breakfast but lunch too.

The food was spread out before them. As Arthur set his laptop to the side, he asked her about Charlie. Stuffing her face while answering him, she realized the man was a good attorney. He seemed to know his shit.

After telling him about the accident, as well as the names of the people that had worked there, she got up to find the file she'd left here with her brother in the event she could ever get him an attorney.

"This will be very helpful. I have it here, too, that

your parents had filed for a wrongful act, naming the daycare as negligent. Do you know if anything became of that?" She told him that they were turned away from every attorney they asked for help. "This isn't the way I do things, Ms. Jefferies. I get to the bottom of things regardless of what someone might want me to do."

"My parents did try." He told her he wasn't saying they hadn't but that the attorney should have done it regardless of if there was money or not. "Yeah, there isn't any of that either. I know Mr. Anderson said he'd pay you, but I'd like it if you were to send me the bill. I don't have a job right now, but I can work anywhere and do a good job."

"I'm sure you give every task all you can when assigned." Even after all the food was eaten and leftovers put away, they talked. It was nearly nine at night when Arthur stood up to leave. "You've given me more than I think I could have found in files for this. I'll be by in the morning to pick you up. I'm staying at Caleb's tonight, so I'll be close if you think of something."

"I don't know what else it would be. I think we've covered about anything and everything." She smiled when he laughed. "I'll see you in the morning."

After he left her, she found her old bedroom that she used when she came to stay with Charlie. There was very little in the room. An empty dresser. A closet with hangers that looked like a row of flowers. They were so colorful. Finding one of Charlie's large shirts, she pulled it over her head and laid down on the bed. Tomorrow was either going to break her or let her start over. She wasn't sure she'd get either, but it was a hope.

Gracie thought of her family. Her parents had tried so hard to make their lives better. They were making some headway into having money put away for a few things, like a vacation, when Charlie had been hurt. They'd not been able to take any vacations, of course, but they had always made time for their children.

In the summer months, they'd have picnics at the local parks. Go fishing at the dam. A great many free things that seemed like the world to them. A large basket of treats, Mom's jams, a ham sandwich or two, and a bottle of water was their meal when out like that.

Mom made quilts for their beds. Dad could repair anything and everything. That was where most of the extra money had come from was Dad knowing how to fix something. Everyone in the neighborhood knew to take it to Dad to be repaired, while Mom knew how to take something in and let it out when it came to clothing.

What they didn't have in material things, they certainly had more than enough love to go around. Twice that she could remember, they'd taken in a child or two. Just until their parents could find a job. Mom babysat, too and helped with tutoring.

Everyone that came in contact with them respected them and liked them. They were the best. Now she was the only one left, and it made her sad to think that when she died, that would be the end of the Jefferies that she was related to.

Turning over on the bed, she looked out the window that was at eye level. Even for as late as it was, children were playing outside. She rarely saw a kid where she'd been working without a phone attached to their ear or looking down at it. The kids were catching firebugs. They weren't keeping them but catching and then releasing them. Gracie had done the same thing when she'd been little.

Remembering to set her alarm so she'd get up in the morning, she turned her phone back on. Always surprised that it would come on, she set it for seven. Not bothering with the messages she had on it, she watched the children more. They were much more entertaining than anything that Billows had to say to her.

Charlie had been gone for a month now. The woman who came in to check on him had called her one morning, sobbing about how he'd fallen asleep and not woken. Even as she tried to calm the woman down, Gracie felt her heart shatter. It was the hardest call she'd ever taken.

In that month, she'd been working herself to death to be able to afford a ticket to come here to do this last thing for him. Affording the ticket to come here for his funeral had nearly bankrupted her. But she'd made do with eating her free meal at work and taking any leftovers home that the cook had saved for her.

Then Billows found out about the free meals. The next afternoon there was a sign put up that there would be no more freebies for anyone. She'd been the only one that qualified for the meal, as she was the only full-time waitress there. Not because she was scheduled to be full-time, but covering both Billows' and the day manager's schedules when they decided to just not show up was the only perk she got. He'd also taken her overtime away from her.

Gracie had almost stopped doing the job of three people when she realized that if the place shut down, which she was sure would happen, there would be a lot of people out of work. There were seven waitstaff as well as kitchen help, cooks, and the busboys that depended on the place having their doors open. She couldn't have done that to anyone.

Every week she'd get paid for thirty hours, what she'd been scheduled for, and all the other seventy-plus hours would be free. Not that she didn't keep track of the hours she wasn't being paid for. She wrote every shift down, and even the extra time she had to do at home by making schedules, ordering food for the place, having carpets replaced when needed, and repairs done, as well as a lot of other jobs the manager should have been taking care of.

Gracie had been working there for ten years. She knew the place better than the people who had built it, she'd bet. Gracie was upset about the things she'd been doing and how she'd been treated. Pulling her mom's quilt up to her nose, she inhaled deeply of the scent that was still there. Sunshine. It calmed her more than anything else.

It was nearing midnight when she felt she might be able to close her eyes for a few hours. She really hadn't slept well since she'd gotten the call about Charlie being gone. Crying herself to sleep, she let the tears fall while she willed herself to sleep.

Chapter 1

Gracie wasn't sure what was going on, but she had four people sitting with her on her side of the long conference table. The other side had twelve. What the hell was going on? She kept asking herself as well as Arthur every time she could whisper to him. What the hell were all these people here for?

Bickerton and Bickerton had called this meeting for this afternoon. After showing up at nine yesterday morning with Arthur, the people working in the office, not the owners, hadn't a clue about not just the meeting but that she'd gotten herself an attorney. Allen Bickerton, as well as his father, James Bickerton, had been upset about the meeting and that no one in the office had been told about it.

The meeting had been set up the night before with the father of James Bickerton, Howard. However, when they'd shown up, the attorneys decided that they had more important things to do than to come to a meeting so early in the morning and didn't show up. They had told their secretaries to reschedule for one today. Gracie just wanted this over with.

At a quarter until two, the two men came into the meeting room. Howard Bickerton had been in since eleven thirty and was embarrassed that his son and grandson hadn't been in on time. Finally, he'd had to call them at home and then send a police officer to each of their places to bring their asses in. His words, not hers.

"I don't know what this is all about, father. Nor why you think you should be involved. Mrs. Jefferies was told that she must come here and settle up her husband's estate then we'd be finished. Any junior attorney that works here could have had her sign the paperwork that was left for her, and we'd not have to bill anyone these extra hours." His father corrected James. "So? Brother. Husband? It doesn't matter. She just needs to sign off on the paperwork left for her, and things would have been finished with us."

"I'm glad that you brought this up, Mr. Bickerton." Howard told Arthur to call them all by their first names so there'd be less confusion. The other two looked disgusted with the idea. "All right. Thank you, sir. James, I'm concerned with the paperwork that you thought to have Ms. Jefferies sign over for this firm. The wording here is what I'm speaking about."

"Do you know how large this firm is, Mr. Fowler? We're big enough to be all over the United states with offices in Europe as well as Canada." Arthur asked what that had to do with anything. "I'm telling you this because you're just too small to take on a company the size of ours. Just have your client sign the damned paperwork, and we call all call it a day."

"She'll need this reworded here about the money being paid to you and this firm from any lawsuits you have taken out for my client." Gracie was handed a sheet of paper, and while she read over the script there, Arthur continued. "I might be new to this sort of trickery, but it sounds to me like you've decided that if she gets around to suing someone on her behalf. I'm thinking that it's the daycare that caused the eventual death of her brother Charles Jefferies that you and your firm get all the settlement. Is that what you're telling me in this paperwork?"

"I haven't any idea what you're talking about." James looked at his son before having a seat. "We put this in the paperwork all the time when there is a wrongful death lawsuit pending."

"You told my parents three times, that there wasn't anything that would make you take on the accident of my brother because there was nothing to go on. Are you saying that you waited until he died before you decided it might be worth your time? Not to mention, you'd just do it without my knowing so that you could take all the money from it. No wonder attorneys are called bloodsuckers. You two are the worst of the worst, preying on the people that you should be helping. You fucking bastards. You would have gotten away with it, too, had not Mr. Anderson stepped in."

"Caleb Anderson? He's helping you with this?" She nodded her answer to Howard without taking her eyes off the two men across from her. "Well, well,

James, I do believe this young lady is a good deal smarter than you thought she was. Oh, and I know of your little plot now. Christ, when Rose Beth told me about what the two of you were up to, I didn't believe her. Didn't think that the two of you would be...damn it, boys, you're going to go to prison for this."

"For what? We didn't do shit wrong, old man." Gracie couldn't believe that Allen was calling his father that, having so much disrespectful for the elderly man. "It's not like she could have afforded us in the first place. We're just doing what should have been done decades ago. Making the daycare center pay for their part in the death of Mr. Jefferies."

"Mr. and Mrs. Jefferies, both now deceased, came to Bickerton and Bickerton when they found out that their only son was gravely injured at the same daycare they paid to watch over him years ago. He'd sustained head injuries that affected his wellbeing, his life as well as his mental state to the point where instead of living a full life, it was cut short from the damage sustained when he was hurt. It might well have taken him twenty-four years to pass away, but an autopsy was done on his body, and it says that the damage that was done to him as a child was the reason that he died so young. The coroner decided to make sure that everyone knew that his death was murder and stamped it as so." A copy of the death certificate that she'd been trying to get for weeks now was put into her hands. Arthur handed copies of it to all fourteen people on the other side of the table. "Mr. Jefferies didn't get the help that he needed to make sure that he was able to live out his life in relatively good health. All chances of his doing so were taken away from him by the two of you and other law firms when the elder Jefferies came to you asking for help. It is my pleasure, James and Allen Jefferies, to tell you that as a representative of Gracie Jefferies, the only survivor to his family is suing you personally as well as the law firm that you both own."

"Bullshit." She looked at Allen. "You don't have the balls to sue us. Not to mention the other eight firms that they went to."

"You knew that this could happen? That my brother would die from his injuries?" Allen laughed and said that even an idiot like his grandfather could see that he was going to be a retard after that fall. She stood up, as did Arthur and two other people that were on her side. "He wasn't a retard. He worked hard on becoming a good person. He had to keep to himself because loud noises bothered him. He—how could you do this to my family? How could you sit there, like greedy fuckers and wait for him to die so that you could profit from his death? And if you disrespect your grandfather again, I'm going to knock you on your ass."

Howard put his hand over hers and thanked her. James and Allen laughed at her. When she sat back down after only rising a few inches from her chair, the door behind her opened. Not turning around to see who it was, Gracie felt her entire life, all the terrible things that she'd had to endure, hit her in the heart. These men took her brother away from her. Took his life like they had hurt him in the first place.

The two of them were taken away by the police. She sat there without seeing the things going on around her thinking. When someone touched her hand, she looked into the face of a stranger. She then looked around the room. Everyone was gone but the woman with her.

"My name is Tabby Anderson. My husband is

Caleb." Gracie told her what her name was. "Nice to meet you, Gracie. I'm here to clear up a few things for you. First of all, all the other firms have been arrested too. At least the ones with names on their doors have been taken in. Your mother, she kept very good notes when it came to what she was doing with your brother, didn't she?"

"Yes. She even passed the book onto me when— how did you get it?" Tabby told her. "I guess I might have forgotten that I gave it to him the night he was at my brother's home. Arthur read it all and realized that it was more than he'd thought he was taking on, I guess."

"Yes. All of us read it to get to the bottom of things. Some of this information that we had for today was there for us to just make happen. Like the firms that your parents went to that week. Who she spoke to as well as the times and dates. Everything we needed to know in that she was turned down at every avenue that she tried. The autopsy that was done on your brother was done the day that he died. It's required when someone dies alone. I'm so profoundly sorry for your loss, Gracie." She thanked her. Then she looked at her. "Something you're just remembering?"

"You said you were Caleb's wife. He's off his rocker if you ask me." She laughed. "Yes, I can tell that the two of you must get along well. Mr. Anderson laughed at everything." Gracie looked around the office, standing up to go to the widow, when she saw that clouds had rolled in.

The pretty park that was below her was beautiful. There were flowers everywhere one looked. Hanging and planted. The larger trees even had benches around them, and there were several people sitting in them while waiting for the rain to come in. Children were still playing out in the warm weather too.

"Charlie was such a wonderful little boy. My brother and hero. We played so much together. We'd read books to one another all the time. I remember once when we were in the yard playing when we found a dead bird. We asked mom for a box, but all she had was a tin can that we used by sealing up the end with tape. He and I were going to be something someday we used to tell one another." She paused, thinking about memories that she had of Charlie after he was hurt. "Sadly, that's about all the memories I have of him that are good. After he was hurt, it was difficult for all of us, Charlie nor I, to had anything close to a normal life after that, of course. Mom and dad worked so hard to keep him home with us. I honestly think it had to do more with him not being with us at home rather than not being able to afford it. Not that we could. I'm not sure that anyone expected him to be as functioning as he was when he got older. Due entirely to my parents working with him daily."

"From what I've heard, he was good at his job too. I had to look up what a line hook was. When I did, I wasn't sure why I never thought of that being a job someone had to do from home." She told Tabby that her brother was handicapped and that he was able to do it because of some program that he was in. "Still. To be able to tie a special kind of knot into line to hold a fishhook seems like a big deal."

"It paid his bills and put food in his belly. I helped him as much as I could. My parents died a few years back, and I was able to sell their home for a larger profit than I could have imagined. With that money, I was able to buy him a home to live in and have it outfitted for him. The care he got, a nurse coming in once a day to check on him, was paid for by the state." She laughed a little. "I thought in buying the house that the two of us could live together and save some money. But he couldn't handle me being there. Not that he hated having me around, but he couldn't cope with the noises and smells of having someone in the house with him. He'd been living with my parents since birth, so he knew their oddities. But I'd moved out to go to college when I was eighteen, and he'd gotten used to me not being around. So I moved to Tennessee and got myself a job. However, that never worked out, either. For different reasons. So I worked at the restaurant that you and your husband owned to make myself some money until I could find myself a better paying job. That was ten years ago. I'm still slinging hash and being treated like a dumbass because I don't have better skills to get me into the big leagues. Not where you and your husband are, but it would be nice to be able to afford pancake batter and syrup in the same grocery shopping week. It wasn't really that bad, but it felt it some weeks."

"You're owed a great deal of pay from the restaurant." She told her that it was much too late for her to get that now. "No, it's not to us. We didn't know anything about the restaurant or even that we owned it until it came up on one of the spreadsheets that we had made for us to keep track of things. When Caleb's mom passed away, there were a great many things that we had to take care of in order to make sure that people were being paid as well as work taken care of. Caleb was so impressed that you ordered food for the place, made schedules as well as took care that the restaurant was spruced up once a year. All on your own, from what we could figure out."

"I might not have called him about the place if not for the fact that there was money missing. He said he'd make sure that it was taken care of, and I figured he'd just brush me off with saying that to me. It wasn't until a few days later that I heard from in town that his mom had passed away. She was someone that people really respected. As I said before, Mr. Anderson is off his meds or something. He laughs at everything." Tabby laughed and stood up. "I'm headed back home in a few days, I guess. I haven't anything to go back to now. My apartment was furnished when I moved in. And since I couldn't afford the extras like basic cable and shit, I didn't own a television even."

"You'll need to stay at least until the court date is set, right? I mean, you'll have to be here in order to have yourself and your family represented. Correct?" She said that she didn't have anything else to do, so she might as well do that. "Yes, then there is the issue with Bob Billows. He's going to be someone that has to be dealt with soon. Common sense, something that I don't think he has a great deal of, isn't a flower that grows in everyone's garden. Caleb was hoping that you'd go there and help him with the confrontation in a few days."

"That's all right with me. I don't mind. I'm not going to work there. Not again." Tabby nodded. "I'm serious. I don't want to run the place. Wait tables or anything else that has to do with Devonshire. I don't want to be sucked in again."

"I don't have any plans of you going back there to work." She shook hands with Mr. Anderson when he joined them in the room. "If you'd be so kind as to go with me, taking along, I'm sure, the notes of what you've done for the restaurant for the past ten years, I'd be very grateful. Billows is claiming — and no, I don't believe him — that he's had to pay out of his own pocket for things that you screwed up. He couldn't tell me what those things were, mind you, but he did mention that it was in the price range of over a hundred grand."

"He's full of shit. Even the replacement of the carpets every three years didn't cost that much. I did get some good deals on other things, too, for the place." Mr. Anderson asked her what they were. "Well, for one, the filtration system cleaned out yearly didn't cost anything. The students at the college used it as their exam final if they could do it at the place. The carpet was costly but laying it would have been more. But that didn't cost anything either. Students again. I was trying my best to make sure that whoever owned the place wasn't pouring good money after bad."

"I'd not realized that — Billows faxed me all the bills he had in his possession when I asked for them. The carpets, according to him, were changed out yearly and at an exorbitant price. Also, he said that you had placed the order for the carpets without thought to making sure that it wasn't too expensive." Gracie told him he should check out where the carpet he had receipts for was placed. "You think that it was his own home that he was billing me for? Christ, the guy is a trip, isn't he?"

"You have no idea." Gracie had handed all the things from the restaurant to Mr. Anderson when he met her at her brother's home last night. He had brought her more food like she was going to starve to death or something.

Gracie couldn't believe that she'd only been here for five days and so much was going on that involved her. Not caring for this sort of life where shit was going on all the time, she wanted and was going to try very hard to get a place so that she could chill out for a few hours and not have to think about scheduling and food prep.

~*~

Martin was enjoying his stay at Caleb's place. However, he did like the peace and quiet of the town better. There was forever something going on at Caleb's home. If it wasn't children running around, which Martin loved, there were people going in and out of the house for one thing or another at all hours of the day or night.

Well, it wasn't that bad. Some days it would be

quiet around the house because both he and Tabby weren't there. Then there was the phone. It was constantly going off with someone wanting Caleb to invest in whatever ideas they had. Nothing was off limits, either. There was one person that had a wonderful idea that would take all the dirty diapers from hospitals and nursing homes and use them to plant seedlings in. He supposed it had some merit, but that didn't mean he wanted to have his veggies gown in a stranger's bowel movement either. That was something he'd rather not think about, ever.

Slipping out of the house, he decided to take a walk around town to calm his thoughts. Hearing someone speaking, he looked around for the source. The woman coming toward him was walking like she was on patrol and cursing like she was hating every second of it. He paused in his own walk to watch her take hard strides as she ate up the distance between them. Whomever she was upset with, he would surely hate to be them when she got to them. Just as he was going to make his presence known to her so as not to be knocked down, she looked him in the face and glared.

"Did you know that there are any number of

legitimate reasons for a woman not to trust a man? Many, I tell you. However, when you ask a man why he doesn't trust a woman, he says because they're female. What sort of fucked up messed up reason is that?" She snorted. "Just because I'm female, I'm not to be trusted. That's some fucked up bullshit if you ask me."

She stormed by him using the same stride as she had before, never gotten an answer, if she required one, bitching about how men have all been led to believe that all women are distrusting. He felt the laughter of it all bubbling up from his belly until he had to hold onto the wall next to him and not fall over. Martin saw her returning to him, and she had a glint in her eye that sort of scared him. Standing up, trying to compose himself, he waited until she was in front of him again before he spoke.

"My name is Martin Hamilton." She smacked his hand away. "That was incredibly rude. I'm only being polite to—"

"You laughed at me." He said that he'd found her rant to be absurdly funny. "Why? I just made it perfectly clear that I think all of your kind, men are assholes and need to be castrated before they know how to use that thing between their legs. Some of them still don't know how to use it, and they're perfectly nice guys. But nice guys don't satisfy, I don't think."

"I'm a nice man. I think so, anyway. We could work on your theory if you'd like." Martin wiggled his brows at her. However, she cocked her head at him and glared. "You're very pretty, beautiful actually. And while I think that I should be terrified of you, I can only think about how you walk like all your anger is going to glide you across the sidewalk and that everyone should stay out of your way. Is that about right?"

"My brother died." Before he could tell her how sorry he was about her loss, she continued. "I think everyone in this town knows about it, and they're all telling me how sorry they are. It's been a month since he died, and I do miss him terribly, but nothing is going as I thought it would when I came here to take care of his estate. He no more had an estate than I do a good job or nice clothing. Which I can't find because men, your kind, have been telling me that since I've only lost my brother, I need to take more time for myself and have someone like Mr. Anderson take care of me. I don't need a fucking sitter. I'm a grown assed woman that needs a fucking income. My money is running close to nothing, and I've got an entire town of people being as nice to me as they can. Damn it all to fuck and back. What am I supposed to do with myself?"

"Is Caleb the one taking care of you or his grandda?" She said she didn't know that he had a grandda around. "He does. And a brother. His name is Sheppard. The elder man is Shep Anderson. I just wanted to be clear on that."

"Why?" Martin asked her what she meant. "Why does it matter if it's any of those men? I mean, in the event that you didn't remember, I'm off men for the rest of my life. At least until I get back home. Wherever that happens to be when I get there. Or land there the way things are going. Then tomorrow, I have to travel back to Tennessee so that my former boss, a jackass if there ever was one gets his comeuppance. Whatever the hell that is going to mean to – men, you see. They all have this program inside of them that makes them think that women are helpless and stupid. They should fucking give birth. I've never done that, but I'm thinking that men will think that women aren't as helpless as they think if they tired to piss out a baby from that hole at the end of their dick one time. Men are fucktards."

Martin couldn't help it. He burst out laughing again. She was not just beautiful, but she spoke her mind in a way that had him feeling sorry for her former boss and even Caleb, for that matter. They were both in for it if they tried to treat her like anything but an equal.

"How about a drink of tea or whatever is it you drink?" She growled at him, and he had to stifle a laugh, or he was sure she'd murder him where he stood. "I'm sure from all your observations today, you'll need a nice soothing drink of something."

"You're an asshole." He thanked her, still trying very hard not to end up dead from laughing at her. "I don't have a job; thus, I have no money. I could use a drink, but I don't want to be beholding to you for a buck or two because I'm thirsty. What will it cost me for a glass of something cold? Other than water. I'm sick of the very color of water."

He laughed again, not even caring at this point if this was his last day on earth. He'd not had this much fun in a very long time. Guiding her into the little café that he'd been in before, he was greeted with hellos from Yazzie and Joey's children. They were with their mom. Sitting with them, he excused himself to go up and find a waitress to wait on them. The woman running the long counter said she'd be right with them all.

Returning to his seat, Martin introduced the woman to the people at the table. She, in turn, told them her name. The five children and Yazzie, Joey's wife, had only just arrived to have some lunch. It was Yazzie that told her that she was blind and that her husband, along with Martin, were stepbrothers to Caleb. It was Madison that spoke first. She was nearly as outspoken as the young woman with him was.

"Hello. You're very pretty. We saw you arguing with our uncle a few minutes ago. Mom told us to behave and come in here so that you could argue in peace. You didn't sound like you cared all that much for peace when I heard you. What's a fucktard anyway?" She looked at him, and Madison spoke again. "That sounds like a bad word that could get me into trouble if I repeated it. But you didn't have any trouble like that, did you?"

"No, I have a terrible habit of speaking my mind when I'm upset. Like today. Have you ever been that upset?" Madison told Gracie not only that she had been but why. The look on Gracie's face hurt him to his soul. "I'm so very sorry, Madison, that you and your siblings had to endure that. Having your food taken away from you, along with your blankets, is a horrible way to treat a child. An adult, too, for that matter. You're very brave to have been able to keep the others safe while in your care."

"Thanks." Madison looked at him before looking back at Gracie. "Mine and Michael's mom sold us to the place where we were being mistreated. She was my mom's sister. Mom hasn't done nothing but treat us like the best thing she's ever seen. Who's not treating you that way, Ms. Gracie?"

"I was only ranting about things. Nothing to worry about. Tomorrow it will be something or someone else with me. I just miss my family. My brother died recently, and I'm having a hard time making things work for me." Madison nodded and was cut off from saying anything more when the waitress came to take their order. Gracie stood up. "I'm going to go home and wash my mouth out with soap. If there is any left when I get there. I'm sorry for intruding on your —"

"Please don't go. Please. I'd like for you to stay and have lunch with us." Martin could have kissed Yazzie for inviting Gracie to stay. "I'm sorry about your brother, but I've heard Joey and the others talking about what has happened to your family. Please join us."

"You really should, Ms. Gracie. We can make sure you get to take the leftovers home. If there are any." Gracie thanked Michael for his kindness. "I heard you telling Uncle Martin that you don't have any money or a job. I'm powerful sorry about that. I know what it feels like to be hungry. So if you stay, well, me and the others will make sure you have enough food for tomorrow. Okay?"

"Yes, all right. But I don't want the leftovers. I'll be heading home soon, and I'm going to just stay there. I have to find myself a job, but it's not as bad as I was complaining about." Martin had a feeling that it was far worse than she was saying, but he didn't say anything to the others. When his phone rang, he stood up to answer it, going outside the café to talk.

"Martin, what do you know about short and long-term investments." He told him everything that he knew. Which was a fair amount of information. "Thank you so much. This was much more than I was getting from the internet. Thank you."

"My pleasure. Caleb, I have a question for you. You can tell me it's none of my business, but what do you know about the young woman that is going with you tomorrow to Tennessee? She's here having lunch with Yazzie, myself and the kids." Caleb asked him if he wanted personal information or about why she was going to Tennessee with him. "Both but for now… well, I ran into her when she was ranting about the town. Not so much the town but the men living here."

Martin told him everything that she'd said to him. Also, how broke he thought her to be. Caleb asked him to hang on a moment while he looked and wasn't surprised to hear back from him in short order.

"She's had the power at the house turned off yesterday. Nonpayment of billing. I didn't know. I can take care of that right now." Martin cautioned him about that. Thinking that she'd put him in the group with all men she has today. "I never thought of her not having the means to pay anything that came into the home. Much less getting around town for groceries and such. Christ, I just assumed. Assumed poorly, but that's no excuse. What is it you suggest that I do?"

"Nothing. You might want to figure out a way to lend her some money tomorrow when she goes with you. Say it's payment for her help or something. I'd not let on like it's charity or something. She'll knock your head off." Caleb laughed. "Don't laugh at her. I have to tell you. However, she's had me in stitches since I met her. Come down to the café while we're here and figure something out. Please. She'll kill us both if we don't do this the right way."

"All right. I really do need to get her paid for her overtime as well as her extra duties. I know it's going to be a hefty sum, but I've been so busy with the other shit that is going on that—no excuse. I'll be there in about half an hour." After thanking him, Martin also told him that she wasn't planning to return with him. "Does that bother you, Martin? Her going back to her place?"

"Yes. I don't know why and don't want you reading anything into it, but I've never had this much fun, even before my mom passed away. Even if it's only for some laughs, she's made me feel better than I have for quite some time."

"All right. I'll have a talk with her." Thanking his brother again, he smiled at that thought. All his life, he'd wanted a brother, and now he had two of them with more coming along. Going back into the restaurant, he wasn't the least bit surprised to see George sitting on Gracie's lap and Madison and Carol telling her about their new rooms. Sitting at the only vacant seat, which happened to be across from her, Martin decided that he was going to try and hang out with Gracie for as long as she'd allow him to. Without being a man about it. Martin thought his mom would smack him upside the head if she heard him talking like that. She'd also have a good time, too, having her around.

Chapter 2

Gracie walked through the rubble that had once been her apartment complex. There had only been six apartments. Three up and three down. Hers had been in the middle on the bottle floor. It had been.

There wasn't anything left to even try to save. The people in the apartment next to hers had left a candle burning all night. The melting wax and flame had fallen off the speaker that the candle had been sitting on and caught the curtains on fire. It had consumed the entire complex in less than two hours. Long before the firehouse got the call, that could have brought them out.

"They said that it was difficult to get service out

here with a cell phone." She nodded to Kylie, Caleb's attorney, when she spoke to her. "No one in the house had a landline, and that was why the fire department didn't get here in time to try and save anything. I'm so sorry, Gracie."

"I should have come back days ago." Kylie assured her that there would have been nothing she could have done about it. "I know that, but…well, I'm just glad that I'm here now. This way, I can, I don't know, figure out what I have to do now. Nothing in the place was mine as it was furnished, but still, it was my home for so long."

They had arrived on a private plane that had landed about an hour ago. Even before they were disembarking, Caleb had heard about the apartment fire. She had hoped that there was something that was salvageable, but it was all gone. She had no idea what she might have done had she been here. The way she was feeling right now, Gracie thought that she might well have covered her head up and let the place take her with it. Nothing was going right, it seemed.

"Did you have insurance?" Gracie had told the police that were hanging around that she'd not been able to afford it three different times now to different officers. As it turned out, she was the only renter that didn't have anything to fall back on. Being poor and broke all the time had left her insuranceless as well as homeless. She tried her best to look as if it wasn't bothering her as much as she was feeling. It would be like one of them to find her a place to live and pay it until she died or something. They were much too generous for her today.

"Would you like to hang out here or come with me? I can handle Billows just fine. However, I don't think that being here is going to do you much good. At least with me, you get to blow off some steam." She told him that she was prepared to go with him. "I hope you don't mind, but I got you a reservation at the hotel I'm staying at for the next few days. I know you said you were going to be staying here but, well, this will be better."

"Thank you." She didn't have anything to wear either to bed or to a meeting tomorrow, but she'd be able to take a long hot shower and wash off the smell of smoke from her when she returned here. She wanted to…well, she didn't know what she was going to do, but she had to do something. Either that or she was going to do something very stupid. It hadn't been a good month for her so far.

First, she'd lost her brother. Gracie hadn't been able to get off the day he died nor the few days after to attend his funeral. Having to fly out and back on the same day had cost her all her savings, not that there was all that much, but she literally had nothing to fall back on. Then she'd gotten time off to come here to get his affairs in order, only to find out that the firm representing her brother's death had been going to make sure she got nothing when he died.

Gracie hadn't wanted a great deal of money. Enough to pay for his funeral arrangements. To be able to come out and be there for not just his funeral but to lay him to rest as well. Now, as it was, she was homeless, jobless and had not one tarnished penny to her —

"Gracie, we're here." She didn't say anything to Caleb when he handed her out of the limo other than to thank him. She was afraid really that once she got started on speaking to him — even about the weather — she'd just tell him it all. How she felt, how her heart was broken and that she didn't have a clue on what she was supposed to do now.

The office where she and Caleb were led was huge. There were other people there whom Caleb seemed to know. In addition to Billows, who was blustering about how this was a waste of time, there was his lone attorney that seemed uncomfortable having to be sitting across from Caleb and his five attorneys and herself.

"Mr. Anderson, I assure you that whatever Gracie has told you can only be another lie to make her look better. She's been nothing but a pain in my ass since I hired her." Caleb told him that Gracie had been working there before him. "Well, that was a mistake too. Someone leaving her to work for so many years."

"If she hadn't, then where would my restaurant be, Mr. Billows?" He didn't say another word when advised by his attorney. "Good thinking. Keeping your mouth closed until asked to answer something might be best for you."

The paperwork that she'd given Caleb's attorneys when they asked for it was neatly typed up in a thick stack. Caleb leaned over to her, handing her something in an envelope.

"I'm sorry. I meant to give you this when we arrived, but with all the other things going on, I completely forgot. It's the first three months of your pay from when Billows started working as a manager that you weren't paid for." She nodded, taking the envelope and stuffing it in her backpack. "The rest is coming to you when Martin gets it all figured out, all right?"

"Yes, of course. Maybe I can get me into a place to live when you leave." He looked at her oddly but didn't say anything to her. "I'm not going to be working the restaurant, you know that, don't you?"

"I do. But you're not planning to come back with me?" She shook her head, confused why he'd think that. "We'll speak later."

While she didn't know what the two of them would talk about concerning her living arrangements, the thing with Billows was started. Paying attention to what Billows had to say about her cut deeper into her already busted-up heart. Gracie wondered if she'd ever have a beating heart again after this.

"I have a list of complaints that Mr. Billows had

provided for me about Ms. Jefferies." The attorney for Billows handed her a file with the complaints on them as well. "As you can see, these are dated from the beginning of her tenure with Devonshire."

"These have been doctored." Billows' attorney just looked at him like he knew they'd been doctored and hadn't wanted to use them. But had been made to do so. Mr. Fowler handed them back. "I have these same complaints, but mine are the real deal. And it has Robert Billows as the one they're complaining about. Same message, but I'm afraid you have the wrong person on the complaints."

"They are too about her. Just look at them. It says that she sat up behind the bar and cleaned her nails while the restaurant was busy. You can see that right there. Also, that other one talks about how she was taunting me while I was waiting tables."

"How much is a Salmon En Papillote, Mr. Billows? Or crepes suzettes? Do we have steaks on the menu?" Billows asked her what she was going on about. "You're the one that served these meals, you said. Do you know the prices of these meals? Or even if they're on the menu?"

"We have steaks, yes. I've had a couple of them for my meal a few times. So we do have steaks for those of us that like the simpler things. As for the Salmon thing, I believe you made that up. There isn't anything that — why are you questioning me about prices when I'm the one that made up the menu in the first place." She repeated the salmon thing for him. And said that they did not have just steaks on the menu. "Yes, we do. I've eaten them numerous times. On my break. You're just trying to make me look bad. What do you have to say about that?"

"Nothing at all. All the salmon dish is really, is it is wrapped in parchment with olive oil, sea salt and dried dill. Parchment is a sort of baking paper for cooks. You'd have to know that if you had waited on any tables at Devonshire, as that is the most requested meal on the menu. A house special, so to speak. The only steaks that we provide are chicken breasts that are sliced thin and skewed. Then they're grilled until they're done and served over a bed of rice and fresh fruit and vegetables. Again, something that you'd need to know when waiting tables. Each waitress that I hired would spend a week in the kitchen so that they could understand what they were serving. So that when they're asked a question about a meal or what is in it, they can honestly give a good accounting of the meal. Also, they're required to eat each meal that we serve to be able to make recommendations since you took away employees being able to buy their dinner for half price."

"That's all on you. You were eating at the restaurant twice a day and not paying for it at all. I had to make it go away so that you'd not be getting freebies." She told him why she'd been entitled to the two free meals. "Nope. I don't care how many hours you work a day; you're not getting anything for free. For as much as you pester me when I'm at home, I'd say that I should be able to have as many meals as I want to eat."

"You do have as many meals as you want to eat. You also eat them in the dining room, yelling at the staff to bring you things while they're waiting tables. Like you're a priority over the paying customers." He said that he was. He was her boss. "Then you should have fucking acted like it. You never once made out a schedule, no matter how many times I tried to show you how. Never once did you order anything for the place, despite me giving you the counts and told what we needed to order. Nor did you do any deposits, bank pickups or anything else that had to do with you managing the place. I did it all."

"And a piss poor job you did of it too. Christ, do you know how many times I would come by with friends to have a nice meal, and you'd turn me away? Telling me—your boss, I might remind you—that the place was too busy for me to just pop by. I saw empty tables. All you would have had to of done was push some of those together to accommodate us." She said that they were reserved. "So? I don't get how you cannot just give a table to someone right there when someone else had called in to reserve a table. I was there."

"Yes, but you weren't going to pay either, were you? Paying customers are always better to have in the seats rather than yours and your dozen or so friends." Billows reminded her again that he was her boss. "Yes, and a piss poor job you did of it too."

It was then that she remembered that there were others in the room with them. After apologizing to all of them, she asked if she could be excused. Caleb said he'd like a break as well, and everyone stood up when she did. Except for Billows. Going into the hall, she found the ladies' room across from the conference room and slipped inside. Taking the first stall, she nearly didn't make it after throwing up what little she'd had on her belly since this morning.

Sitting on the floor after washing out her mouth, Gracie let her tears fall. She hated confrontations more than she did anything else. But there were times when it was necessary, she knew. However, today hadn't been one of those times. She should have just kept her mouth shut and let the attorneys handle what had happened. The knock at the door startled her, and she sat there when Caleb came into the room with her.

"Are you all right?" She shook her head. "I could see that. But you handled this case much better than I think the lawyers—blood-sucking lawyers did."

"This isn't the time for you to be funny. I had a fight with a man that doesn't care for anyone's opinions other than his own. Robert Billows is a moron." Caleb agreed with her and sat on the floor with her. "Aren't you afraid of getting your suit all nasty?"

"No. I have other suits, and I'm sure that whatever nastiness there is on the floor will be taken care of by the dry cleaners. You're going to be all right, Gracie. I promise you that." She told him that she knew she would, but it's been a hell of a month. "Yes, I can see that. But you'll be all right once this is taken care of."

She didn't want to argue with him. Gracie knew her circumstances better than anyone. She was in debt to her eyeballs. Not to mention…well, she wasn't going to go down that road again.

"I'd like for you to come and work for me." She told him that she wasn't going to wait tables anymore. She would if it came to it, but that was all she was going to do. Not run the place as well. "I should hope not. But I have a few managers of other places like Devonshire that need to learn from the best. You would be my eyes on the job, so to speak. Go into a restaurant of mine and Tabby's and observe what is going on that is making it lose money. I will tell you that once you started running the one that Billows was supposed to be running, it was the only one that we owned that was showing a hefty profit. Also, the turnover for staff was the lowest count per year as well."

"I wasn't doing anything special. Just making sure that the staff was happy with their job. Also, the perks that needed to be put in place. Most of the people were bringing in their own drinks and food so that they could afford to work there. That was working out really well at half price for them until Bubblehead decided to step in and take it away." He laughed at her calling Billows Bubblehead. "What would I do? Be like this undercover person that would see what they're doing to fuck up your profit line?"

"Yes. Something like that. I'm not sure what the fuck up might be. I've eaten at a great many restaurants in my life; however, I know nothing about running one. My mom might well have been able to tell you, but I'm not that savvy as yet about it. I would like for you to go in and have dinner once or twice and figure it out." She told him that wouldn't work. "I didn't think it would, but I didn't want to have to make you work for this for me."

"Yes, well, if I have no access to the back room where things are, then I might well listen to you about what is going on. I'd get dick information." He asked her if she was ever not blunt. "No. Not when I'm talking business with someone. How I would get into being waitstaff would be easy. I'm assuming that in addition to losing profit, you're also losing staff as well as customers, correct?"

"Yes. One of the places that I'm getting bad reports about is losing a waitstaff person a day. Then there are the cooks. Dishwashers are even difficult to keep around, and I would think that it would be the least likely person to interact with anyone." She shook her head and told them they were the most important bit of information. "Why? What do you think is the reason for them being important?"

"They see the plates. Which means they can see what is not being eaten. I observed those areas too. If a lot of a dish is coming back not eaten, I see whether or not it's too large of a portion. If that's not it, then I look at how much is eaten. If it's half, then I'll go one step more. If it's only a bite gone, then I know that it's the food and not the size. Sometimes while it might sound good to the chef, it's not so much to the person paying and eating it." Caleb said he'd not thought of that. "Because you never get to be on the back end. I'll do this for you, but I want to be able to count on working at least forty hours a week. Paid overtime too. Also, I'd like to have insurance."

"Deal. Anything else? I'm at your disposal on this. You're going to be saving me a great deal of money on losses." She asked him where these restaurants were. "All over the world."

He stood up and put out his hand to help her stand up. Gracie stared up at him before taking his hand. When he smiled at her, she had a feeling that she'd just done something that she might regret. Working for a billionaire because his places to eat were losing money.

~*~

Martin liked riding on the private jet. However, he wasn't so sure that he should get used to it. Today was special, he knew. Flying to Tennessee with Tabby to have dinner with Gracie and Caleb was weird, but then he wasn't as rich as his stepbrother was. He didn't think that anyone was.

"Are you all right?" Martin said that he was just nervous. "I can understand that. I'm not used to this much of anything, much less a private jet that takes me where I need to go at a moment's notice. It's funny when you think about it. We're going to Tennessee to have dinner, then tomorrow, flying back to have dinner at home. Mind boggling to me. Did I tell you that Gracie is going to be working for us?"

"Yes. She's going to be helping with profit and losses at the restaurants." Tabby told him that was right. "While I have a very good understanding of P&L reports, I don't understand why he'd care so much as to hire someone to come in and see what the problem is. Why not hire an entirely new staff or close it down. I'm sure that the two of you can afford it. I'm not trying to be crass here, but it seems that it's like putting money into a car's interior after the engine has blown up." Tabby laughed, and it made him smile.

"It might be a simple thing that the cook isn't keeping consistent with the things that he's supposed to be making. Or that the carpet isn't looking well maintained anymore. I didn't know this, mind you but heard it from Caleb when Gracie told him. She told him to read the reviews. Or better yet, send someone in to have a look around. Perhaps the interior is old and in need of updating. There might be a toilet that is forever out of order. Small things that irritate people enough where they don't enjoy their dining experience and blame it on the food rather than what it really is." He said that he rarely goes out, so he might not notice those things. "But you would. However, you might not know what it was that turned you off from the place and blame the food. That's one of the bigger ones that Gracie told him will get him shut down faster than anything."

Martin supposed that Gracie would have a very good knowledge of the ends and outs of a place to eat. She'd been working in one almost as long as he'd been a stockbroker. He decided that he was going to be more observant from now on, even if it was just a fast food place. So he'd have something to talk about with Gracie.

As soon as the plane landed, they were disembarking. It was only Caleb that met them at the gate, and Martin felt his disappointment all the way to his toes. When they were in the limo, he told them that Gracie was going over the paperwork for her new position and hadn't known that Martin was coming as well.

"I thought she knew." Tabby told him it was

a surprise for them both. "You do know that there is nothing going on between us, right? I mean, we've talked, but we're not dating or anything like that. I'm not even sure that she likes me."

"You like her, however. Correct?" He nodded before he could figure out it was a trap. "Good. That's half the battle when it comes to setting the two of you up."

"Perhaps I don't want to be set up." They both laughed at him. "Look. I don't know that I'm fit to be around people much. Gracie and I have spoken, ,but I don't think we're suited. She's a little bit outspoken, and I'm not."

"If it doesn't work out, then it doesn't, Martin. But I think that the two of you could be having a good time as a sometimes couple more than most people." He wasn't so sure about that and told Tabby that. "You and Tabby have a great deal in common, whether you believe me or not. The one thing that I think that you can do is help each other out of this terrible funk you both are in. Caleb was telling me that she still believes herself to be homeless and broke as fuck. She's not so far as I'm concerned. She can live with Caleb and I for the rest of our lives if she wanted to."

"Caleb gave her the check, correct? That at least should have her feeling a good deal better about her homeless situation." Tabby told him that as far as Caleb knew, she'd not looked at it. "I can see her doing that. Just putting it away thinking that it's not that much as she isn't used to people giving her what she deserves."

"That's what Caleb said as well." They were headed to the hotel when his cell phone rang. It was Caleb. Tabby had been talking to him earlier before they landed, and he wondered what his friend could want from him.

"Gracie doesn't have a cell phone. I was wondering, before we meet for dinner, if you could pick her up one. She'll need one that is on the higher end for working for me. Also she'll need a laptop as well, but we can get to that later. She's really down in the dumps, Martin. Gracie went over to the apartment site after the meeting and has been there for a couple of hours. That's why I realized that she didn't have a cell. I think she's wondering what she's going to be doing now." Martin said that he'd gladly pick up a phone for her as well as a laptop too. "Thanks. You might want to talk to her about what you're finding too about her payroll. I don't know that she thinks she's getting all that much from all this."

"I've gone over the entire first two years for when Billows was in charge, and in addition to the check she has now, you're going to owe her about another hundred thousand dollars for that two year period. She was never paid for breaks, only on occasion, got a day off. In some instances, she worked as much as forty days in a row without any time off. I have to tell you; she was working more as a manager of the place in that last year than waiting on tables. She was only being paid for thirty hours at four bucks an hour. That isn't even counting the things that she did from home to keep the place running."

"Christ. I'm not saying that it's going to hurt me to pay her, but I really wish that I had known this a good deal sooner. She literally gave up her life for that place for nothing." Martin agreed as the limo dropped him off at a place he could get a cell phone and computer equipment. "She'll have a fit if she were to hear me say this but get her a phone with all the newest shit on it. I want her to never be without working for me."

Martin Hamilton   73

"If she's going to do the job that you spoke to me about, you're going to have people trying to take her from you all over the world. This is going to be epic in the restaurant business. I hope you know that." He said that he'd just have to make it worth her while not to leave his employment. "She won't. If nothing else, I've discovered that Gracie is very loyal to someone. Even if they're treating her like shit."

"I don't have any plans of doing that to her." Martin told him he'd better not. "I won't. She's become important to me over the last few days. And being here with her one on one, I can see she has a passion for things working out for the underdog. Some of the things she told me about restaurants and how to figure out what is making them lose money is wonderful."

Martin entered the retail outlet of the company that carried his and Caleb's cells and looked around. They had a great many phones and plans to choose from, and since he'd been given the go-ahead to get her a good phone, he was leaning toward one that would give her an endless supply of data and minutes. Also was good for taking pictures.

The laptop that he was able to get for her was

better than the one he had at home. He would help her with spreadsheets on it. Also, he'd help her with sending things via fax or email to Caleb when she had information. As an extra bonus, he was able to get her earbuds as well as charges for all the things he'd gotten, and a carrying case for the computer. He was nearly ready to finish up when Caleb called him again.

"Can you go by the bank for me?" Martin laughed and asked him if he was thinking of paying him for being his delivery person. "I will if you want. However, I have something more in mind for you. At the bank, there is a company credit card there for Gracie. Another thing she is going to be pissy about. She'll need to stay at hotels and eat when she's not working when she's out there for me. Also, there is a card for you as well. I want you to be able to pay for the things that you're picking up for me. This way you wont be out whatever cost it is going to be for doing this for me."

"I can do that." He asked him to hold on while he spoke to the woman at the cell phone store. "She's going to hold all this until I get to the bank. Which, she told me, is just across the street from here."

"Good. I'm working on getting her car rental discount as that will be something else that she'll need to get around. I don't know what she'll need to be driving, but I'm sure she'll have no trouble telling me about it." Martin agreed with him as he laughed. "Yes, well, she is a good deal more outspoken than I'm used to."

"I find it fun to hear her beating my chops over something." Caleb told him he was nuts. "All right. I'm in the bank. If you think of anything else I'm going to need, please call. Also, I'm going to have the woman at the store program yours and Tabby's numbers in the phone for her."

"Joey and Yazzie's as well as yours too. If there is trouble, I don't want her to be limited to only a couple of numbers to call. I have a feeling that there might be a bit of trouble with her doing this for me." He said he'd take care of that. "Thank you so much, Martin. I hate that I'm making you run around, but you've no idea how much I appreciate you doing this for me. Then when we're in the restaurant, I can give it all to her in a place that I hope she won't cause a scene."

"Yeah? Well, good luck with that. I think she'd

bring you to the carpet no matter what you did to her."
Caleb was laughing as he hung up. The woman at the
store was more than happy to program the numbers
in the phone for him. She also gave him her number.
Deciding that he'd take it just to keep the peace, he was
out the door before he could think about what Gracie
might have to say to that. Shaking his head, he slipped
into the limo that had come back for him and was
headed to the hotel. Dinner was going to be loud and
fun, he thought. He didn't envy Caleb one bit.

Chapter 3

Pounding on the door, Gracie was surprised when Martin opened the door. She took a step back and then looked down the long hallway. He asked her what she wanted.

"I thought that this was Caleb's room." Martin told her that it had been, but the room he'd been assigned at adjoining doors, and he and Tabby had wanted it. "Oh. I guess I'll go find him."

"Come in. I was just getting ready for dinner, and you might as well hang out with me. On the table, there are some things of yours that—"

"Wait. I need to figure out if this shit is right." He turned back to her, and she noticed only then that he was shirtless as well as he had a towel in his hand drying his hair. "Go get dressed. I can wait."

"What is it that you're confused about? I might be able to help you." She said that Caleb had given her a check earlier, and she'd only just had a chance to look at it. "Oh, then you'd be wanting to take that up with me. I'm the one that figured out your wages for you."

"This check is for fifty thousand dollars. There is no fucking way that I was owed that much for a couple of months of work." He sat down at the table that was covered in electrical equipment and moved it all to the side to pull up paperwork on one of the two laptops there. "What are you doing? Didn't I tell you to get dressed? Damn it, you're half naked."

"I am going to get dressed. I wanted to show you what I came up with so you could read it over while I'm putting on my shirt. Also, you'll want to keep this in mind when he pays you the rest of the money that you're owed." He explained to her about how there were several different wages for her to be paid. "You get a wage for being the bartender. And when you're waiting tables and tending bar, there is another wage. It's all here. When you were doing the job of the manager, even working from home, you get an entirely different wage. Ordering and scheduling will also be in that wage."

"What's this number at the end of each marked wage?" Martin explained to her that was her overtime wage for each job. She looked over the spreadsheet for a moment before looking at him. "This must have been a nightmare for you to figure out. What will Caleb say when you tell him that in one week I didn't get paid for...." She had to run down the column of numbers. "There is no way that I should have brought home a fourteen hundred dollar check for that week."

"That's without overtime too." She read over the numbers, comparing them with the numbers that she'd written down in her notebook. There were a lot of times when she'd been doing three jobs at once. However, she never thought that she should have been paid the higher wage while doing it. When Martin joined her some twenty minutes later, she was still staring at the check that Caleb had given her earlier. Martin sat back down in the chair he'd vacated. "Are you all right?"

"I don't think so. I can't believe that in five years' time I was working this much. Some weeks I noticed

I was working as many as a hundred and sixty hours with only eight hours off for the week." He said that so far, he'd seen where she'd done that seven times. "I saw that. I got triple time for anything over sixty hours. Then five times my pay with anything over one hundred hours worked. I bet that not too many restaurants have to do that too often."

"I had to look it up and then talk to Caleb about it. After digging through some of the paperwork that he and his mom had put together for every business they own, he told me that he needed to update the amounts of overtime. He thought there should be a break too at eighty hours."

Shaking her head, she was still sitting there when there was a knock at the door. "Are you expecting someone to come here?" She said that she'd ordered a dress to wear tonight at Tabby's insistence. "I bet you'll look lovely in it. Here, you can look this over too while you're here."

The cell phone wasn't one that she'd seen on television. It did everything. Since she'd never owned one before, she only looked it over without touching the buttons. Messing up Martin's phone would be just what broke the camel's back.

When he told her that her dress was here, she took it from him and headed back to her room. Martin stopped her to hand her the phone. Gracie told him that it was very nice.

"It's yours." She shook her head, backing away from it. "It won't bite you. Just take it. With working for Caleb, you're going to need this to be able to contact him when you need to. It will also track you in the event something were to happen to you. From what Caleb told me, you're going to be working in different countries, and he wants nothing to happen to you."

"This is too much." He told her that if she were working for him, he'd want her to have the best as well. "They have phones in the hotel rooms."

"Speaking of which, you have a credit card as well." She didn't want to touch it either. "You're going to need it to rent cars and hotel rooms when—why the hell are you always so stubborn? Just take it so that we can both know that you're as safe as we can make you."

Gracie took the phone and card and made her way back to her room. "Mother fucking men. They think that I'm so helpless. Fuckers." Picking up the phone in her room, she called the dress shop that she'd gotten the dress from.

"Hello. My name is Gracie Jefferies. I was wondering if it's too late for me to change my mind about the blue dress." The woman told her that she'd send it right up. "If you'd not mind putting the necklace that you said I could borrow with it, I would really appreciate it."

"Pissed you off, did they?" She laughed with Holly, the woman that she'd spoken to earlier. "Well, I have another dress here that will make them sit up and take notice. I'm going to bring it to you personally. We'll make them regret treating you like you need them to lead you around on their arm."

"How did you know that's what they were doing?" She said that in her business, men did that a great deal. "Well, I have to be ready in half an hour. Can we fix this up by then?"

"Oh honey, in ten minutes, I can have you looking like a cake topper at a bachelor party. You just wait and see." When she closed the connection, she wasn't sure if she was lashing out just a bit too much.

It wasn't until Tabby showed up to get help with a zipper—because Caleb wouldn't keep his hands to himself—that she told her what she was doing. Rubbing her hands together, Tabby said she wanted to help. After that, Gracie was ready to turn the tables on the men.

The men were going to meet them in the lobby. After getting dressed up, Gracie wasn't so sure that she was making the right move. She looked a little hookerish, she thought. But Tabby and Holly assured her that she looked like a wet dream. Gracie wasn't sure how that was any better, but she thought that she did look nice.

The men were in the lobby first, and she was glad for that. She didn't know how she felt about her dress anyway, and if she had time, she could still change into the blue one. Holding onto the railing until she got herself walking better in her heels, she looked up in time to see Martin looking in her direction.

Turning just enough to see that Tabby was behind her, she just wrote off him looking at her like she was a meal. It had to be Tabby. She looked beautiful in her all-black dress with slits up the sides. Martin came toward her when she picked up her handbag from the boutique where she'd gotten the dress from. He held the little bit of a purse so that she could put her new credit card in it as well as her cell phone that she could not see a use for.

"Is this a statement dress?" She glared at him. "If it is, I'm hoping that I'm reading the statement that you're conveying. Christ, you look amazing. To say that you're wearing a red dress does not even cover it. It's everything about you and it."

"What statement are you reading from this dress? That I'm not a bimbo? That I'm a good deal smarter than you think, or for that matter, any man thinks I am. I'm not stupid." Martin told her that he never thought that she was. "Then why did you treat me that way in your hotel room?"

"Because if I didn't have you bickering at me then, I would have tossed you up on the table and taken you right then and there. But this, taking this dress off of you if you'd allow it, is making me hard as stone and greedy to know what it is that you're wearing under this." Gracie told him that she wasn't wearing anything and walked away. It was a stupid conversation, anyway. What did it matter what she had on under the dress. It left very little room for things like panties and bras.

He was still standing there with his mouth hanging open like a moron when the limo pulled up in front of the hotel. Caleb told her that she looked beautiful and didn't ask stupid personal questions about what was under the dress. She was nearly to the limo when Martin put his arm around her waist. Looking up at him, she could see something in his eyes that she'd never seen on a man before.

"I'm going to try and be very good tonight." She asked him what he was talking about. Martin stared at her for a moment. "You have no idea, do you? You don't see that every man in this lobby is adjusting themselves. Their cocks are stretched out painfully, do you, Gracie." She glanced around the room and saw that everyone was looking in their direction before looking back at Martin.

"It's just the dress. It's very red." He kissed her. It was more like he was showing possession, that he owned her in some way. Before she could tell him that she belonged to no one, he spoke close to her ear.

"You are the most incredibly sexy beautiful woman I've ever seen. Not only that, but you have an innocence about you that makes me want to shield you from every man in the world. It's not fake either, your look. You genuinely have no idea just how gorgeous you are right now." She looked at him when he stood up again. "Gracie, you were always beautiful to me, but right now, you're more beautiful than any words I can say that would come close to your beauty. It's not just the dress, love. It's you in the dress. No one in the world could have pulled this dress on their body and made you look like you do right now."

"You're confusing me right now." He said that he knew that and was sorry. "I'm not sure what to think about this change in you. I only wanted you both to see me as a person. I am, you know."

"You are. A brilliant woman with a very good head on her shoulders with just enough naivety that will make men beg to be around you. If for no other reason than to say that they'd been around greatness." She snorted at him. "And there is my Gracie. How about we discuss this later when we get back from dinner? I might have more to say to you then."

"I hope so. Because right now, I'm not sure what you're talking about." They got into the limo, and she had a moment of panic when she had to slide across the seat for Martin. But she was saved when she saw Tabby do the same thing. She simply lifted her dress up to slide with her butt. It didn't pull her top down, exposing her breasts as she thought it would have.

Dinner was wonderful. She was able to try things that she'd only served before, and she enjoyed it all. The relish plate, a long bowl-like setting filled with celery sticks, carrots, as well as green onions, olives and pickles, something that was simply brought to the table to be munched on, was better than having bread put out, she thought. It was also not as filling so that people would finish their dinner without being too stuffed from the bread.

As appetizers were brought to them to sample, she was excited to try the stuffed mushroom, a Devonshire favorite but decided that, in the end, she didn't much care for them. The sausage was overpowering, and she didn't care for the greasiness of the mushroom. But she was delighted to try the other items that had been ordered.

Martin ordered for her after requesting him to do so. While she was very familiar with a menu, she'd been sort of jaded on what offers there might be. When asked if she liked steak or not, she told him that she was in the mood for seafood. He ordered for them both as he liked seafood as well. Tabby started talking about the things going on at home as soon as the waiter had left them.

"Yazzie has been teaching anyone that wants to learn sign language this week. On the first day, she only had about ten people there to learn. The next day she had nearly fifty. I guess that there are a great many people wanting to learn a second language. She's also going to teach Spanish to some of the people around town too." Tabby explained how Yazzie could hear a language and know it in just a few seconds. "Her kids have picked it up better than the adults have, so they've been helping her after school."

"How wonderful for her. I know ALS too. My grandmother was blind from birth. I never understood why she wanted to learn how to speak with her hands when she couldn't see them. She said that it gave her an advantage over most people as that she could talk to the deaf as well. Most of the time, she would only put her hand on their hands to understand them, but she was very comfortable with learning how to speak for them." Tabby said that was what Yazzie would do as well. "Most of the time, people hear that someone is blind or deaf and don't know that they could be one or the other. Grouping them in one lump makes it so that she can relay messages from them to speaking people."

"I'm glad that you said it that way. Yazzie is having a wonderful time helping out at the hospital as well. Her being able to speak different languages has made communication there helpful as well." Gracie glanced at Martin, who seemed to be listening to the conversation but not participating in it. Caleb was doing the same thing. Finally having enough, she asked the two of them what was going on.

"I'm not sure what you think is wrong with Martin, but I've been trying to think of a way to tell you something. This evening just after we left the hotel, there was another fire set about a mile from your complex. The same couple that had the candle burning that caused the fire to go up at your place happened there. Three people were killed." She asked Caleb if it had been arson. "They're saying that it was deliberate. But since lives were taken, the couple has been taken in for questioning. They've been arrested, according to Kylie, who is keeping tabs on it for me. They're trying to blame it on you."

"I don't understand. How is that remotely possible?" It was Martin that asked the question of Caleb. "She wasn't even in the state when the first fire occurred. How are they going to say it was her fault?"

"They weren't aware that she was out of town until they were told in jail." Gracie leaned back in the chair. She thought that she'd gotten along well with all her neighbors. It wasn't until Caleb spoke again that she realized what working for Caleb was going to get her. "You won't be questioned about either fire. If it ever comes to that, you'll have attorneys with you at all times. But I don't think anyone will connect you to either fire once they know that you were working for me when both fires occurred."

"Is it because of your money?" He looked like he didn't want to answer, but Caleb finally nodded. "I see. I have to ask you something. If I had been a part of the fires, would you have made it so that I wouldn't be questioned because of my employment with you?"

"No. I would have turned you in myself if I had any suspensions of you being in either of the fires." She thanked him for that. And was grateful when Martin took her hand into his. "You're welcome, Gracie. And I'm happy that you aren't upset that I'd turn you in."

"If I fuck up and cause the death of something or even just fuck up, I expect to be treated like everyone else. I would hope that you'd question me first and treat me fairly, but I have no doubt that you would." He thanked her this time. Then she thought of a conversation she'd had with the couple once. "I just remembered something about them. Once, they told me that they had lost everything in a fire some years ago. It might behoove you to have a look into their pasts. This might be an ongoing thing for them."

After thanking her, he pulled out his cell and called someone. Gracie looked at Martin. He was staring at her with an odd sort of smile on his face. "I'm sorry for being a bitch to you earlier. I shouldn't have said the things that I had to you." After kissing her on the mouth, he told her they were just fine. Dinner was much noisier after that.

~*~

As soon as Caleb and Tabby stepped out of the elevator, Martin pushed Gracie into the corner and kissed her as the doors were closing. Giving her all that he was feeling, Martin ran his hand down her thigh, then up to her ass and cupped the firm muscle there. He pulled back and looked her in the face.

"I want to take you right now, but I'm sure that there are cameras all over the place in here, and they're waiting on the show." He took another step away from her when she moaned. "Right now, with your bruised lips and nipples hard, I'm ready to say fuck it and show them how much I want you."

"Not yet." He nodded and went to the other corner of the elevator. They only had two floors to go, so he pushed the buttons to their floor. The stop before their floor had a couple walking in with them. Martin didn't move, nor did Gracie. She was still breathing hard, and he was simply hard. The couple, older than the two of them by a bit, turned and smiled at them both. The man winked at him as if he knew what was going on with the two of them. It was embarrassing for him but more so for Gracie. No longer leaning against the wall, she was out the door when it opened again, and he followed her. She was standing outside her room when he was able to catch up to her.

"Gracie?" She turned and looked at him. Tears in her eyes. "Oh honey, nothing will happen if you don't want it to. I swear to you that I'd never do anything to harm you in any way."

"I know that." She fumbled with her key card, so he took it from her to let her into her room. When she continued to speak to him as she entered, he followed her, locking the door behind them and laying the key card on her purse that she had put on the little table. "I've had sex before. A few times. However, I didn't much care for it. I have been thinking for the last couple of hours off and on that it would be different with you. That you'd...I know I'm babbling but let me say this. All right?"

"Yes, of course. I've had sex, too, and while I did enjoy it, it never really felt all that satisfying. It will with you. I'm sure of it. The few times that I've kissed you have made me feel like I've never felt before. No pressure on you, I promise you, but I wanted you to know that." She thanked him and kicked off her shoes, making her several inches shorter than she'd been all night. "You really have knocked my socks off tonight. Not only with your beauty but everything there is to know about you."

"You don't have to butter me up." He walked to her slowly, giving her time to tell him to stop if she didn't want him touching her. After touching his fingers to her delicate cheek, he wiped away her tears and told her how smart she was as well. "I've never felt all that smart. Sexy, either, so I do thank you for that."

She laid her head on his chest, and Martin felt as if he could take on the world in that moment. When she asked him if he could just hold her for a few minutes, he would have held her forever, denying himself food and water just to give her what she needed. Finally, after a few minutes, she looked up at him. Kissing her gently on the mouth, he guided her to the couch. When she stood up after seating, he did as well.

"I would like to just chill out and watch a movie with you." He said that he'd go to his place and change. "Wait for me to change, then we can settle in at your place for tonight. Also, we can order some snacks. I'm not hungry, but I love popcorn with a movie. Is that all right with you?"

"Yes." While she went into her bedroom to change out of her dress, he called room service and asked for a charcutier to be brought to his room. Also, some popcorn that they could cook. When the lady at the desk asked if they wanted drinks, he had noticed that Gracie drank water all the time and ordered several bottles of water to be brought up. After hanging up, he sat back and waited on Gracie to be ready to go to his place.

He didn't have long to wait. She came out of the bedroom in a sloppy sweatshirt and shorts. Her knee-high socks looked like something he'd wear, and he laughed when she showed him her fuzzy slippers that had the head of a cat kind of creature on them. He took her hand into his as they made their way to his room. He was changing into something similar to what she had on when he heard the door to his room being knocked on. Knowing that Gracie would handle it, he also brushed his teeth.

The tray that they brought up was almost too lovely to eat. It had all kinds of meats on it as well as cheeses. Fresh fruit and veggies accompanied it in trays on the side. There were bottles of water in a smallish cooler filled with ice that had him laughing as well as several serving forks, knives and cheese cutters. He was eating a couple of the carrots while she went to pop the corn.

Finding a movie for them to watch wasn't nearly as hard as he'd thought it would be. She hadn't been to a movie theater in ten years and had no television since she couldn't afford it either. There was a TV at the restaurant over the bar, Gracie told him, but it generally only played whatever sports were in season. He hadn't been to a movie in a while either, so he was glad to see a few things on the list that he wanted to see. Settling down to watch a sci-fi flick was good for them both.

Martin was surprised that when the movie was over that they'd eaten nearly all the tray that had been sent up. Even the fruit, which was Gracie's favorite thing to snack on, looked decimated. They'd gone through about all the waters too. Straightening up the mess, he watched as Gracie helped him. She made no move to go back to her place, and he didn't bring it up. As she stood up and stretched, he stood still, waiting for her to make the next move.

"Can I sleep with you here?" He nodded, feeling stupid when she laughed. "All right. Do you want me on the couch or in the bed with you? Naked."

He leapt over the little coffee table they'd been using as their table and fell over the footstool that she'd been propping her feet on. Reaching out to grab her, taking her down with him, he was careful to roll with her so that he took the brunt of the fall. He nearly asked her if she was all right when he realized that she was laughing hysterically. Martin couldn't help but join her.

"It's doubtful to me that anyone would have referred to you as graceful, have they?" She laughed all the harder when he told her that he was usually up to perfect form. "Ah, so it was me giving you a choice as to where I slept that got you all fumbly."

"No, it was the naked part that made all my blood rush from my head to my cock and made me stupid. I guess in that moment, I thought I could fly, and I'd take us both to the bedroom to get you naked quicker." He laughed when she did and when she turned to look at him, Martin told her something that he had only just realized. "I love you, Gracie. I think I have since the moment that I saw you. I love you with all my heart."

"I love you too. I don't actually know when that happened, but I've fallen in love with you too. Saying that, I want you to know that at any time you get tired of me, all you need—" Martin kissed her silence.

They laid there on the floor for several moments just kissing and talking. When he felt like he could get up without falling on his ass again, he stood. Then he bent and picked her up from the floor. Holding her in his arms, Martin carried her to the bedroom and was thrilled that someone had come in and cleaned up after him. He'd been a mess before getting ready for dinner, and he'd had to give himself several pep talks to keep calm. Which meant, too, that he'd changed his shirt several times and showered as he sweat himself to near dehydration.

Lying her gently on the bed, he stepped back. The need to take her right then was overpowering, so he calmed himself as best he could. It wasn't until she sat up and pulled her sweatshirt off her head, baring her nakedness to him, that he knew that they were ready for this. He was going to make love to the first love of his life and knew too somewhere in his heart that she would also be the last love of his life too.

Chapter 4

Reaching for Martin, he asked her to wait. When he pulled his shirt up and over his head, she sat on the side of the bed to help with his pants. He had to adjust his cock before she was able to unbutton the first button on his jeans. The rest of them just popped loose as she made her way down the line. She noticed that his cock was just peaking from his boxers, and she leaned in to kiss the tip.

"Christ, love. That felt wonderful." He helped her pull his jeans down to his thighs. Pulling his boxers down, she took his cock into her mouth and laved it with her tongue. His hand at the back of her head was comforting, but he was rushing her, so she removed his hand. "I'm going to come if you keep that up."

She didn't care at this point. He was filling her mouth over and over, and she loved it. Sliding her tongue down to his balls, she cupped them into her hands while tasting him there. Every sound that he made fueled her to do more for him. Making her way back up to his crown, she took him deep into her mouth and swallowed him down past the tightness of her throat. Whatever she had expected from that wasn't what she thought she'd get from him. His shout that he was coming had her swallowing quickly. She wanted the tightness to make him do just what he said.

While she wasn't able to taste his cum this way, she enjoyed his fucking her mouth. Her own body was hard with need, too, so when he pulled from her mouth, she felt the pop of it just before he pushed her back on the bed and got between her legs. Christ, if he touched her even with his fingers, she was going to come. He tore her shorts off her, shredding them so that he could get to her. In moments, less than two heartbeats, she was screaming out her release as he suckled at her clit.

"Again." She obeyed his command, wondering if she would survive a night of lovemaking with this man. As her body seemed to be revving up for another huge climax, he slid his fingers into her, stretching and making her feel like he was fucking her. She came three more times as he ate at her pussy like a starved man.

She was no longer in control of her body. Gracie had come so many times now that she was weak. But just out of her reach, she knew that she'd not had the one that was going to put her over the edge. Or kill her. She wasn't sure that she might not wish for death the way she was feeling right now.

When he stood up, she could only stare at the man before her. His cock was standing straight out from his body. There was creamy cum dripping from the tip. His muscles were stone-hard, and he looked like he'd been carved from stone. When he spoke to her, asking her to move up on the bed, his voice was as hard as his abs. Moving to the middle of the bed, he leaned down and kissed his way up to her breast and then to her mouth.

Tasting herself on his mouth was exciting for her. It was as if she was getting a treat that she'd never had before. When he slid into her, she was so wet that it was an easy task. She cried out another climax just having him inside of her.

They'd both had come several times by now. So when he began to make love to her, she was all right with the pace he was making. His fingers slid over her breasts, her arms and her ribs. It was like he was waking her body up just for him. When he started to move faster in and out of her, Gracie wrapped her legs around his thighs to keep up with him. As soon as he stiffened above her, his body bowed back in what seemed like a painful position; he came roaring out her name and his love for her as he emptied himself inside of her. In the last seconds of his climax, her body seemed to have realized that it was her turn. All of a sudden, she came feeling like her body had been turned inside out. Digging her nails into his back, somehow thinking she needed to hold onto Martin and his love, she came a second, then a third time as Martin joined her over and over again.

When she woke, they were both still in the middle of the bed. Martin was still atop of her, so she tried to roll him off her. Not only was he heavy, but she needed to pee in the worse sort of way.

Every time she was able to free herself from

under him, he'd pull her back into his arms. Finally, she shook him awake enough that he looked at her with one eye open. Telling him her dilemma, he let her go but not until he kissed her.

Running to the bathroom now, she tried not to moan too badly as she discovered her body was nothing but a pulled muscle. After washing her face and hands, she returned to the bed to find that Martin had made it so that the two of them were not sideways in the bed but going to be in it correctly. After snuggling up to him and getting another kiss, she closed her eyes and fell back to sleep.

A ringing woke her this time. Reaching for the phone, she pulled it to her ear just as Martin was asking her who it was. It was Caleb. She'd answered Martin's phone, apparently.

"I was looking for you." Sitting up in bed, her face heated up from the apparent humor in Caleb's voice. "I have a list of things that I'd like to go over with you concerning you working for me and Tabby."

"I'm not up yet." He said that he kinda of guessed that when she answered Martin's phone. "Here, talk to him while I get my bearings. Also, if you tell anyone what happened here, I'm going to hurt you."

Caleb was still laughing when she shoved the phone at Martin. He didn't seem any more awake than she was, so she got up and moved to the bathroom to shower. However, her body hurt more than it did earlier, and it took her a few deep breaths before she felt like she could move again. She turned on the shower before she remembered that she had nothing to put on.

"Fuck it. I'm sore." The water was wonderfully stinking to her tight and sore muscles. Standing under the hot spray, she let it roll over her while her muscles began to feel better. Reaching for the only bottle of shampoo in the stall, she was washing her hair when the door to the shower opened, and Martin joined her.

"Caleb said that he'd met us for lunch in an hour. I had no idea that it was so late." He scrubbed her back after finishing up her hair for her. "I don't know about you, but I think I'm broken in places that I didn't realize had bones in them."

"I know what you mean. Even my ear lobes hurt right now." They were both laughing, and she scrubbed his back for him. He was holding onto the wall while she made short work of his back and nice firm butt when she asked him what Caleb wanted. "He said that he'd been looking for me. I feel stupid that I answered your phone."

"Don't be. I think he thought this might happen. I love you, Gracie." She kissed his shoulder and told him that she loved him as well. "This isn't going to be a one-night stand, is it? While my body is too sore to think about making love to you again right now, I'd very much like to wake up with you beside me all the time now."

"I'd like that as well. However, you take all the covers, so we'll have to figure out boundaries from now on." When they both stepped out of the shower, they continued taking care of each other's needs. She dried his back, and he hers. Even her legs and feet were dried by the big fluffy towel that he used. "I don't have anything to wear. I know that we're going to be using this room for the rest of our stay, but I don't know how to get to my stuff."

"I'll go over and get what you need. Then we'll both pack your things up and bring them over here. One thing that I should mention, I don't have a house for us. I was to pick one out when I arrived, but I've been staying with Caleb and Tabby since I arrived." She asked him what he meant by picking out a house. "Caleb knew that he was going to be bringing his brothers home, so he purchased five houses for us to live in when we arrived. His claim was that he'd get to know us all, and we would each other. I just haven't had the energy to do it until now."

"Are we talking just a regular home or one that I'm going to need breadcrumbs to find my way around? The one that Caleb lives in is huge." He said that he'd been given a list of the homes, but he'd not looked into them yet. Martin handed her the file as he left her to go to her room. She was still looking over the specs of the houses when he returned with her things.

"You certainly made it easy for me to get your things. You'd not unpacked anything." She told him that she'd not known how long they were going to be there. "Yeah, I guess I can understand that. I like to unpack so that I feel like I have some control over the room I'm staying in. I got your things from the bathroom too." She thanked him and then showed him the houses.

"This one has nine bedrooms, and it's the smallest

of the four left. The second one, one that I love by the way, has ten bedrooms. I've not gotten to the other two yet, but I'm really liking the second home." He took the pictures of all four of the homes. "The third one is pretty, but I'm not thrilled about having to mow all that lawn."

"We'll get a couple of kids to do it for us." Martin handed her the fourth home pictures. "This one has a pool out back, a pool house and also a large eat-in kitchen. It has ten bedrooms as well, but they're more modern than the others. I love to swim, and it would be nice to have our own pool. However, if the second one is all right with you, it is me too. We can always have a pool put in at any time."

As the two of them made their way down to the dining room, they talked about the houses. She was falling in love with the fourth house and the pool. The grounds were beautiful as well. The eat-in kitchen was appealing to her too. To be able to gather in the room that would smell so wonderful was very inviting. Caleb stood up when she and Martin approached the over large table that he was sitting at.

"I've been looking over some of the paperwork

that I got from the restaurant. I was wondering if you could explain a couple of things for me after you order." She was suddenly starving and ordered a huge lunch. Martin did the same but not the same thing she had. It was going to be fun picking off of each other's plates, she thought. Their salads were brought out right away, and she was munching on hers while she explained the rotation of orders she had made. "I didn't know what kind of money there was to be spent on foodstuffs, so I would alternate meat with the other staples. Most of the time, with the cooking staples, I'd have Mr. Gordon tell me what he would need for two weeks in way of flour and items like that. Then I'd make up a weekly menu of specials, give them to him, and he'd tell me the amount that I'd need to order to make it work. We were really good working together too."

"I can see that. There seemed to be little to no leftover meats that had to be tossed out from the weekly inventory you kept." She nodded as she finished up her salad. "I also love the fact that you cut down the salad dressings to four rather than the ten or so that it was there before. It was a good selection too."

"Most of the others were being tossed out. And

when there were only four to pick from, it made it easier on us waitstaff to be able to tell people what we had. The house dressing wasn't asked for all that much. And it didn't seem to bother anyone when I took it off the list. Most of what I was doing to help me, and the other waitresses was to cut down on the amount of crap that we had to remember nightly." He asked her what that might have been. "Well, we had a nightly special of fish, chicken, pork and beef. Then there were eight to ten side dishes that were basically variations on rice, pasta or a potato dish. The menu went from looking like a study guide with a dozen pages to a sheet that could be printed up weekly and save time. They were cleaner too."

"I like that idea." She asked Martin what he saw he liked. "Well, if the menu is overwhelming, and it can be at times, I'll order something on the first page rather than have to wade through all the pages that might have a better meal, but it's too much. I also like the idea of having only one or two side dishes than having to deal with all the others. I've heard it said from people that talk about huge menus that they can't believe that a single cook, even with a lot of others working with him, that they don't believe that cooking all those meals will make them good. I don't know that for sure. I've always enjoyed my food when I eat out. However, I don't make a habit of eating out, so I could be jaded."

They talked about the other things on the list that Caleb had questions about. He did stop off business talk when their meals arrived. Biting into her roast beef sandwich, she put it down without being able to swallow it. Spitting it into her napkin, she flagged down their waitress. Neither man said a word to her as she complained about her food.

"First of all, I'm not mad. But this had mayo on it, and I requested that I didn't want it on the sandwich. Also, there are green peppers on this, and it made no mention of them being on a roast beef sandwich. I don't care for those either." The waitress rolled her eyes as she picked up her plate. Gracie put her hand on her wrist and told her she wasn't finished. "There is more wrong with this meal than there is right with it. You shouldn't be rolling your eyes at me as I've been nothing but polite about my issue."

"If you don't like the meal, then I'll take it off

your bill. No biggie to me." She looked at her hand still on her wrist. "You can let me go now. I get it that you're not happy. I'll just take it back and eat it on my own. That way, nobody cares."

"Why wouldn't anyone care that my meal is wrong back in the kitchen." She rolled her eyes again. "You do that again to me when I ask you a question, and I'll have you terminated. See? I'm still not raising my voice at you even though I could. I'm going to go back to your kitchen and talk to the cook. There isn't any way that he'd not care about how I'm not happy with my meal."

"He won't give to shits if you want to know the truth." Gracie stood up, and so did the men with her. "I don't think he'll be all that happy if you bring all your men back with you. I mean, we all know that you slept in someone else's room last night."

She'd not meant to slap the girl, but it happened before she could think of the consequences of her actions. Marching to the kitchen, Martin followed her while Caleb detained the waitress. She was hopping mad and threatening to call the police. Caleb was handing her his phone when Martin followed her into the kitchen.

To say that she was appalled by what she saw when she walked into the kitchen would have been an understatement. Telling Martin to call the health department right now had her glad that she'd not eaten any more than she had of her meal. The mess back here was enough to make her belly lurch. It actually did a few times after finding the 'cook.'

~*~

Caleb laughed every time he looked at the health inspector. Mr. Fastener was writing down everything that Gracie was telling him and wiping his brow at the same time. The police arrived just before Mr. Fastener had, and they were taking turns going out in the fresh air in the front of the hotel.

"Are you listening to me?" Martin put his hands on Gracie's shoulders when she looked as if she was going to lose her cool again. She'd done that twice now, losing her shit over everything that she found. The manager of the hotel was apologizing to the guests that had been dining when they had. He was begging them to stay while things were cleaned up. Caleb thought the only way to clean this mess up was to burn the place down. Hotel and all. He doubted that there was any coming back from this.

There had been rats on the sink where the dishes were supposed to have been washed. Meat was warm as it sat out on a counter behind the cook station. According to the billing that Gracie had unearthed under the pile of paperwork on the desk said it had been delivered yesterday. Even the boxes of chicken breasts that had come on the same delivery were on the shelf to the right.

Roaches were scrambling out of the way of the police, that was arresting everyone in the kitchen. The staff couldn't understand why having a little bit of bugs around was anyone's business. Even the walk-ins were filled with vermin that were making nests in some of the fresh vegetables as well. How it had gotten this bad was anyone's guess, but it was about as bad as he'd ever seen, even in third-world countries.

The floor was so slick with blood and other shit he didn't want to think about that he stayed in a position to only have to look into the place to know that he might well catch something if he were to enter. However, watching Gracie handle the things that were going on gave him hope that he'd hired the right person to keep his own restaurants from looking like this. It wasn't until the FDA showed up that she ripped into them about the inspector that had been here just last month and needed to be hunted down and made to eat from here. One of what he thought was a seasoned officer went outside and puked for about ten minutes before he was able to return. Even then, he looked green.

"Mr. Anderson?" He nodded at the man in charge of the FDA. The U.S. Food and Drug Administration took their job seriously. "My name is Agent Petersen. I'm in charge of his mess. I'm sorry. I should start over. I have a direct call from the president. He'd like to talk to you. Please?"

Taking the cell phone from the other man, he waited on the president to finish talking before saying anything. Wilhelm Davis was a good man, and his mother had been right in making sure that he got his ducks in a row to run this country. But what this had to do with him was confusing to Caleb.

"Caleb, I'm sorry about that. I just got off the phone with your wife. She could be your mom's double when it comes to getting things done." They both laughed. "She called me when she heard about what was going on in the kitchen there. Can you elaborate? Actually, I was hoping to talk to your girl Gracie, but I'm told that she's a little busy knocking some heads together."

"You should see her. Christ, oh mighty, I think my mom would have been here cheering her on. This is a mess, Wilhelm. It's a small wonder that no one has died from eating here. Not to mention—Christ, I just don't understand how it got this bad here. This place won't last after this. Even closing the kitchen for good won't help the hotel at all." He said that he had figured that. "They've arrested everyone, even going so far as to go to some of the people's homes that were off today and arrest them as well."

"There have been two deaths from food poisoning so bad that there was no saving them. One was an elderly man the other was a toddler. I'm having the reports sent to Petersen as we speak. Gracie has helped a great deal in this mess, you know that, don't you? I'm thinking of putting her in charge of the FDA and having her have some heads roll over this. Do you think she'll take it?"

"I haven't any idea. Right now, I'd not ask her. She's about as pissed off as I've seen anyone before. Not to mention, she is making sure that every detail is being written down that she's found here. I believe the man she's talking to is going to run out of paper before she's finished here." They both laughed, and Wilhelm said that he'd talk to her later. "You should also know that she and Martin are a couple. I'm not sure how long it will last. However, I'm thinking that they're a perfect match for each other. Martin has been keeping her calm enough so that she doesn't hurt anyone. It's funny to me when I think about it. Martin came to us seemingly a broken man. Depressed enough to attempt suicide. But here he is calming a woman that is hell-bent for leather to murder a lot of the people working here."

"I'm sure that they'll last. From what I've heard, they're a perfectly matched couple. I have also heard from other sources around. The hotel manager has been paying off the inspectors that came around for a good review. He'll be going to prison for his part in the death of the two people that we've found so far. After this, it's likely that a great number of people will be coming forward soon to tell what happened to them at the place. I know you're all staying there, but if I were you, I'd get out. Don't even bother paying the bills. They're not going to be able to do anything about it after this hits the paper." He said that they'd do that now. "Good. All right. I just wanted to give you the heads up on those couple of things and see about what you think of Gracie running the FDA for me. I'm thinking now that she's going to turn me down. She strikes me as a hands-on sort of person, and she won't get that working from an office."

"I've hired her to go undercover to my restaurants and find whatever she can to make sure that they're up and running better. She's a slam dunk at it. I'm seeing firsthand that she can handle herself and others if it comes to that. However, I'm going to have Martin go with her to calm her in the event that things go wrong. Also, since he can carry a weapon, it might keep her safer if things get out of hand like it has here. This place...all I can tell you is that I'm so very glad that I'd not eaten anything here. Including today's meal. I don't even want to think about how long this has been going on."

After closing the connection, he handed the

phone back to the man who had brought it to him. They were not recording the things that Gracie was pointing out, and it was working so much better for everyone. When she walked away from the inspector, he had a moment of worry. But all she did was walk up to him and ask him if he'd please find her another place to stay for the next few days.

"How about we head home?" She nodded, and when Martin wrapped his arms around her waist, Caleb smiled. "I'm glad to see that the two of you are together. You seem to be perfectly matched for each other. I couldn't be happier for the two of you."

"Not that we need your approval, but I do thank you—I'm sorry. That was rude. I'm so upset right now. I don't even want to take my things back with me. It'll be dirty to me, and I'd have to burn them or something. Can we just go now?" He nodded and asked Martin about his things. He told him that he only needed his laptop, but the rest was replaceable. "Good. I'll get in touch with Tabby, and we'll head out. We need to make a stop, however. I'm feeling nasty myself now that you mention it, and I'm going to get me something new and clean to wear and dump this stuff. All right with you guys?"

They both agreed with him, and when Tabby joined them without her things, Martin decided to just run up and get his and Gracie's computers. Once they were gone, Caleb called his credit card company about the mess at the hotel and said he wanted it taken off his bill. They were glad to do that for him.

As they were walking out the door, he noticed that the lobby was full of people checking out. Bypassing the desk, he started telling people to just leave. The place would be closed down before too much longer. The line out the door was longer now than at the front desk. The hotel manager and staff were being arrested just as Martin joined them. Christ, this was a shitshow, and he wasn't sure that he was glad to have a front-row seat to it.

They stopped by another hotel to change and shower. They only got one room as they weren't staying the night and then went shopping. It was easy to get things just to wear home, and after having a shower, he felt a good deal better. None of them were hungry, of course, so they headed to the plane to go back home.

"This was nothing that I ever thought would

happen at a hotel like this one." Caleb told Gracie that he'd not either. "If I find any of your places like this one, I'm going to shut it down so quickly that you'll need to find me to figure it out. I won't tolerate things like that going on in a kitchen. And to find out that the entire hotel was in on it makes me positively ill thinking about it."

"You've no idea how much I agree with you on this." They were headed home within an hour. By the time they were there, they'd gotten hungry, and the four of them decided on a nice grill out. Steaks on the grill and sides were the perfect ending to this day. After they left, Martin called him and asked him if the deal on the houses was real. "Of course. Have the two of you found one?"

"Yes. The one with the pool. I think that Gracie and I could live very happily there for the rest of our lives." Martin paused and then laughed a little. "We were wondering if you could put it in both our names. But Gracie Hamilton. She's agreed to marry me. Also, just do what you did with yours and Joey's. Make it filed, and we'll be happy about that."

After closing the connection with Martin, he told

Tabby what the conversation had been like. She was, very rightly, so thrilled that they were together. Caleb went to bed that night as happy as he could have been. Things were coming together. Now all he needed to do was find the other three brothers, and everything in his life would be hunky dory, as his mom used to say.

Life was going along better than he'd thought it would. And Caleb couldn't help but thank his lucky stars that he'd had the best mom in the world. While he missed her a great deal, he was able to think about her without hurting. She would be so happy with the way things were turning out that he couldn't help but smile thinking about her now.

Chapter 5

Joey looked over the paperwork that he'd received this morning again. Something wasn't adding up. Sebastian Gerald, another brother of his, was off the grid. He'd just simply disappeared from the shelter that he was living in with his sister. He could find her; Daisy Gerald was now living in a school nearly halfway across the world, but her big brother had gone from staying in the shelter for six months to nothing.

"What's up?" He looked up at his son Michael when he came into the room. His son. His children. Joey couldn't get enough of hearing or saying that to someone. "You're looking sappy again. What did I do?"

"Nothing. Nothing at all. I was thinking about my brother." He asked him if it was Caleb or Martin. "No, this is another brother. There are six of us in total. But Sebastian has disappeared. I can't find him. And Caleb and I were going to go and get him in the morning."

After explaining everything that he'd been able to unearth about the elusive man, Michael asked him about the sister. He told him that she was in a boarding school in Switzerland. But he couldn't talk to her without permission.

"Yeah, well, that never stopped you guys from talking to someone you wanted before." Joey almost agreed with him but decided that Yazzie would murder him. "You told me that he was living in a shelter. With his...what's her name anyway?" He told him. "So now this Daisy person is in a boarding school, and he's gone. What is a boarding school anyway?"

"It's a school that you sort of live in. Children live in the houses or dorms while getting a good education." He asked if that cost a lot. "I would think so. Especially since it's pretty far away from here."

Joey pulled up the name of the school and

whistled. He'd not done that before, and now he wished that he had. Showing it to Michael, the two of them looked at the picture of the activities that were available for children that resided at the school. Michael asked him if he thought about sending them there.

"No way. I like having you guys around all the time." Michael looked relieved, and he let it go. "I wonder how he can suddenly afford this. I mean, according to this, it's just under a hundred thousand a year. She's ten, so that's a few more years of this place if she's going to be going there for a while."

"Maybe he won the lottery or something. Or maybe Grandma Abby found her first." Joey looked at his son and asked him why he'd think that. "Well, I hear you guys talking all the time about how generous she was. Maybe like Uncle Caleb says all the time, she saw a need and took care of it."

He didn't have any idea how long he sat there, more than likely with his mouth hanging open, thinking about what he'd been told. He'd bet his life on it that even Caleb hadn't thought of his mother being the reason that Daisy was being boarded at a school so far away. Getting up, he found Michael and the others in the kitchen and kissed Michael on the top of his head.

"You, my dear son, are brilliant. I'm going to go and talk to Caleb now." He was both thrilled and sad for his children that they couldn't find their parents for them. But that only meant that he and Yazzie got to have all five of them. He thought that they were doing as well as they were simply because they were all together. Leaving to find Caleb, he was happy when he was with Martin when he pulled up in front of the town hall.

"We were just talking about you." Joey was getting used to the bear hugs that Caleb gave them each time he saw one of them. Martin would cringe a little, but he, too, was getting better at hugging back. "What have you been doing this fine morning? Martin and I were talking about Billows and his woes. The idiot is trying to find a way to get me to pay for him an attorney so that he can sue Gracie for getting him into trouble. For, get this, being a better manager than he was."

After talking about Billows for a few minutes, Joey asked Caleb about his mom perhaps doing what Michael thought. He was a little taken aback by the thought, but he could see that Caleb thought that she might well have done that. He told him the cost of the school and how even though he'd said that he was working with the FBI, they wouldn't give him anything.

"Not even if she's working for her education or was it paid. They'd not tell me who put her there either. I understand that it's a privacy thing. However, they're tighter lipped than any branch of the service I've ever seen." Caleb asked him about Sebastian. "He's dropped out of everything. No hits on his social security number. I can't find any sort of driver's license. It's like he's been erased from the face of the earth. Even his service record has been locked from me getting to it."

"I wonder why?" Joey told him that he'd been trying hard to just see what branch of the service he'd been in, and he couldn't get into the file. "This is nuts. I might have to make a call or two to figure this out. Have you had any luck in finding the other two? I know that the last known address for Daniel that we had was a bust. Any information on Harlin?"

"He's making his way here. I haven't any idea

what that might mean, but I have a feeling that he's working his way here by doing odd jobs and hitching it. Mr. Grump, the last place that he worked at when I was able to track it down, said that he was living in the shelter while working for him. Harlin was washing dishes but had moved on after getting his third paycheck. He didn't think that he had a car or any means of getting around."

"On his way here from where?" He told him that Grump's Diner was in Colorado. "Christ, that's a long walk if that's about all he's doing. I can't imagine that he's eating all that well or getting enough rest, either. He could be really sick or worn out by the time he makes it here."

"I figure that in a couple of days, he might be in Kansas. That is if he doesn't stop for a three week period working for someone. That will still be a lot of walking before he even gets to the next state of Missouri." Caleb agreed with Martin when he pointed out how much longer it might take. "What if we have the police watching out for him. We know about what route that he's taking. We can go down there in a couple of days and see if we can find him. You said to me last night that he was traveling the larger interstates. We should be able to narrow it down to where he might be coming from."

"I like that plan. I don't want to spook him, but I do want to find him and bring him here." Caleb looked at him. "What do you know about him personally? I mean, obviously, he's alone, right?"

"Yes. He has been for some time. His mom never married after Harlin was born. However, she didn't want him either, it seems. Martha left him with her mother when Harlin was about six years old. She'd been keeping him since his mother had given birth to him, but since Martha decided that she didn't want him at all, her mother adopted him. Grannie was a bitter and mean old bitty by all accounts but seemed to really love Harlin. When she passed away about five years ago, she left everything to him, despite having her daughter, Harlin's mom, as well as three uncles. They, as you might well understand, didn't take that all that well."

"They took it from him." Joey said that they were trying. "So he has whatever she left him and is still walking to where he needs to. What is it that I'm missing? I'm sure that it's something important."

"Grandma Bentley had a good deal of land and money stashed away all over the house. She also kept very good records as to what her children owed her too. None of them thought that she had a pot to piss in, so they never bothered with her after they thought all the money was gone. It seems to me that none of them had any idea that she owned about fifty thousand acres of good land either. Also that it had three very good drilling sites on it. They didn't bother Harlin either, thankfully. Mrs. Bentley and Harlin had it all worked out on what he was to do." Caleb laughed, and Joey knowing the story laughed with him. Martin sat down and enjoyed the tale with the two of them. "When she passed on, Harlin was to sell the land to the highest bidder. Since it was already in his name, he could do that well before the will was to be read. He made a killing off the land and, from what it appears, gathered up all his money from the house and left. The other people named in the will were notified that Grannie had passed on and that they were mentioned in the will. However, by then, Harlin had taken off. Just as, from what his attorney told me, he was told to do. To get as much distance between himself and his relatives as he could before he returned from someplace far away to read the will. As you can imagine, the others are pissed that they can't find him. Also, and this one gets me the best, the house has been demolished, so they can't go there and live while they're waiting."

"Are they all broke?" Joey told Martin that they were. Especially the oldest. "Counting on his mommy to leave it all to him, I'm betting. Even though they didn't know she had anything."

"Even ten bucks would be something for these people. Martha, Harlin's mom, is a druggy. Even before Harlin was born, she was doped up all the time. Lucky for him, she gave birth to him while in prison. That's how her mom had ended up with him in the first place. There is no telling what Martha might have done with him had she been anywhere she could have sold him off." Caleb shuddered at that. It was Martin that asked how much money he might well have. "Over a hundred million. That's just from the sale of the land. I don't have any idea what they had stashed around the house. But I have heard that she had been renting out the land to other ranchers out that way, and that might be where some of the money came from. We won't know until we find him."

"So, let me get this straight. Somewhere out there is our brother, Harlin, *walking* from Colorado to Ohio, perhaps with a hundred million dollars in cash on him. However, he stops places, doing odd jobs for money, then moves on after that." Joey nodded at Martin. "He also stays in homeless shelters where I presume that he showers and cleans up daily."

"I would imagine that is about right." Martin said that he didn't understand. "Would you, looking for someone, think that he'd be walking anywhere? Even in his day and age?" He shook his head. "Would you imagine that a man walking, looking dusty and shit, working at washing dishes would be carrying around all that cash? And we're only assuming he has it on him. It may well be in a bank someplace. But still, he does have that much money."

"Okay, he's hiding out in the open." Joey said that was what he was thinking. "Hiding in plain sight. I guess that's smarter than buying an expensive car, driving it out here stopping at hotels along the way. This way, he's not really leaving any kind of paper trail. If that's the case, how did you find him?"

"I have a friend or two from the service that is helping me. Otherwise, I'd be as in the dark as his family is." Joey was happy that Harlin was taking things carefully. Money, especially a great deal of it, could make people do really stupid things to get to it. The very fact that Caleb made no effort to hide his wealth scared Joey at times.

Caleb did take precautions but not enough to suit him. He wanted him to have guards around him at all times, and Caleb wanted to be approachable. Being approachable could mean your death too. He was worried about his family now that he had one and didn't want anything to happen to any of them. His cell was ringing when they decided on getting some lunch. Since he didn't recognize the number, he answered the call with his last name only.

~*~

Harlin wasn't sure that he'd dialed the wrong number again. Telling the man on the other end of the call his name, he waited for a few seconds before speaking again.

"A man by the name of Caleb Anderson was

trying to contact me. However, the number that I was given was for an attorney by the name of Fowler." He said that was the name of the attorney that was trying to contact the men that had been sired by a man by the name of Berkley. "Yeah, that's the man's name on my birth certificate. My mom and he were an item for a long time. Then he had her send me off to military school when I was about eight. From there, I avoided them both as much as possible. Is this about the books? Or does this have to do with something else with you trying to contact me?"

"Books? I never heard anything about a book from…I, as well as a few other men, have the same sire as you do. Caleb, just after his mother passed away he found out able the others that had been raped by this man, and he's looking for them. I do know that your mother is still alive. But other than that, I've no idea how to contact her, nor you, for that matter. You'd be the only one so far that has their parent still living." Harlin said that he didn't have much in the way of contact with her. That she'd been in an asylum for the last twenty years. "I'm sorry to hear that. But I'm a half-brother to you as well as Caleb and a few other men that we're trying to contact."

"Why? I mean, it's been decades since I was born. Why are you just now getting around to it?" Harlin knew that he was being harsh, but he wasn't in the mood to bring up shit after all this time. "I'm not sure what you think can come of this, but I'm happy with the way things are for me. Berkley is dead and not knocking me around anymore. Which I'm sure you know all about. My mom…well, she's safe where she is now that he's not in her life and leaving her alone."

"None of the others of us that I've been able to speak to knew Berkley other than the fact that he had raped our mothers and left them. As for the book, I'm assuming that it has something to do with your life with him. Or perhaps mentions any of the other women that he raped. From what I've been able to find out, Harlin, you're not doing too well yourself. You've been out of work for nearly four years. According to the resources that I have, you're suffering from chronic depression, as most of us are. You're bouncing from shelter to shelter until they tell you to leave. Through no fault of your own, but they don't want to have long-term people there." Harlin wanted to hang up, but the next thing that he said intrigued him. "Caleb is in a position to help you, and he really wants to do whatever you need to make your life better. In any way possible. You need only come here and meet with all of us then, while I'm not sure what you want to do after that. I do know that any of us have no hold over you."

Harlin thought about what the man was saying. He knew of them. All of the babies born from Berkley. Mostly it was the women and how he had stocked them for weeks before taking them. His own mom had begged him not to leave her, to make her place his so that he'd come back to her. Their relationship, even before he left home, was only violence and screaming at each other. But that was the way his mother had wanted it. To be—

"Harlin, are you all right?" He told Joey that he was thinking about shit that he and the others might like to know. "I know that we would. As I said, all of us have lost our mothers. I'm sure that whatever you can give us will be something profoundly helpful."

"I don't think you're going to say that when you read my mom's diary. She still writes in one at the place she's at. They hand them off to me once or twice a year. Also, you should know that I'm no better off with my mother than the others are without theirs. She was sick before I came along, and Berkley fed into her way of life." Joey said that he was sorry, and it felt sincere too like he meant it. "Berkley lived with us, as I said. I don't know how long he was a part of her life before I noticed him. Then when it was clear that I wasn't going to be lying for him or her again, I got tossed aside. But I do have her books. And you're welcome to read over them as much as you wish. As I said, I don't think you're going to like what you find. I know that I don't like it when I get a new one from her. However, I don't know how much of it's true." He paused for a few seconds before plunging on. "In the first few books, it has how the two of them stalked your mothers. How my mom would follow yours around until he got a pattern all worked out on when to take them. I don't believe that she had anything to do with the actual rape, but she is just as guilty as he is for what happened." He waited for Joey to tell him that he'd changed his mind and that there was no way that he was going to be a part of their big happy family. It only just occurred to him that Harlin really did want to be with them. To be a part of something. So when Joey spoke, Harlin was braced for the blow.

"I'm so sorry for you, Harlin. My heart aches for you knowing what sort of person he was and that you had to endure that." Harlin felt the tears fill his eyes. As Joey continued, he had to lean back against the wall in the kitchen so that he'd not fall to the floor. "I'm going to talk to Caleb and see how long it will take us to get to you. Don't be surprised if you're greeted at the door with a bunch of new family for you."

"Did you hear what I said to you? That I knew about what was going on through the books?" He said that he'd heard. But he also knew that he more than likely suffered more than any of the rest of them had. "Oh, Joey, you've no idea. None."

Harlin was thirty-nine years old, and he was sitting on the floor of his kitchen, sobbing and holding a towel to his face like he'd done as a child. The towel was much like he'd had in his blanket, what that he'd use later to tend to his wounds.

Babbling now, telling Joey all the little things that he could remember. How his mother would hold him down so that Howard could beat him. How, to this day, he couldn't feel emotions like other people. Nor could he, Harlin thought, allow people to get close to him for fear that they'd emotionally destroy him.

"When Caleb and Tabby found me, I was holding a gun in my hand to end my life." He could hear the pain in the other man's voice, and it made him think that he was a kindred spirit. "Tabby took the gun from me and put it to my forehead and told me that she'd end my life for me if that was what I wanted. It wouldn't bother her to do it as her prints would be on nothing. She told me later that it hurt her to her soul to have said that to me. And every single minute of every day, I find that I love that woman for what she did more than anyone. And I, because of her, have a wife and five of the best children ever. Please say that you'll come here with us? Please? We'll leave within the hour to be there."

After giving him his address and a good number at which to reach him, the two of them spoke for another half hour. When he hung up with Joey, Harlin sat there on the floor, sobbing like a small child. Something he'd not done in a good long time was have a good cry for himself.

The place that he was staying in was in a place of flux. It had been his mother's place when he'd been in the military. The very one that she'd shared with Howard when he'd been alive. Boxing up the crap, because that's all most of it was, had been easy for him. He'd not been back here for any reason since he'd been a boy of six. There were no good memories here, and he was tossing everything.

Howard had been killed a while ago, but it looked as if his mom had been waiting for him to come home like before. There was still some of his clothing in her closet. Shoes lined up at the door for him to use. Even in the pantry were things marked with his name on them. Harlin remembered not being allowed to touch any of his food, for he'd bought it for himself. Which had been a lie. Mother had bought everything for the two of them.

Packing what little he'd come here with, he was glad now that he'd washed up his clothing last night and had dried them earlier today. He still used the same duffle that he'd had in the service with markings on it from all the different places he'd been to while serving his country.

Making the call for the donation service to come and get the things that he'd promised them, Harlin helped them load all the furniture into their vans. A couple of the men that had come had stayed to help him wrap the mattresses and box springs in plastic to be put out with the trash.

The food had all been expired by the time he'd gotten around to coming here, and that too went out to the trash. By the time he and the realtor were going through the house, Harlin was about as emotionally exhausted as he'd ever been. He turned toward the driveway when he heard someone calling his name. Being engulfed in strong arms nearly took him to the ground again. Holding onto the man as he said he had him over and over, Harlin had an overwhelming need to never let him go. When he did let the man go, he was embraced by two more men while the first man, Caleb, introduced him to everyone that had come with him.

"My name is Caleb Anderson. You know Joey. This is his wife, Yazzie." He was gripped hard by her as well as Joey and loved every second of it. "This is Martin and his wife, Gracie. Like you, Martin is our brother. That beautiful lady to their right is Tabby, my wife."

They all hugged him several times, and there were a lot of tears shed. He took them into the house with him and was sorry that he couldn't at least offer them a glass of water as everything had been taken away. None of them were upset by his lack of planning, it seemed. It was Joey who asked if this had been his family home.

"I guess you could call it that. My mom lived here with Howard right up until he was killed. I was sent away when I was barely old enough to tie my shoes." They all told him how sorry they were for that. "I've put the house on the market, but there won't be any proceeds from it. The home that my mother will be staying for the rest of her days will take all of it. She's getting the care that she deserves, and after I finish this up, I'm not going to be around for her anymore. Not that I was for some time now, but that's all water under the bridge, as the saying goes."

"Do you have another place to stay? I've made us all reservations at the hotel here in town and one for you as well." Harlin told Caleb that he'd not thought beyond getting this mess taken care of. "I can understand that. Not that my mom left me a mess, but it was nice to be able to get out of our home and into something else. Too many memories."

"Yes, but I'm betting that yours weren't nearly as bad as mine are." Caleb told him he was sorry. "No. I'm the one that should be sorry. I'm a little on the tender side when I think of my childhood. I shouldn't take it out on you guys. Not until I get to know you better."

Everyone laughed, and it was a sound that he thought he could get used to. However, as he was standing there, listening to others about their trip here, Tabby pulled his arm to her and lifted up his sleeve to look at the scars there. Then she did the same thing to his other wrist.

"Don't do this again, please?" He just stared at her. "You're my brother as much as the others are, and it would break my heart to know that you didn't come to me or one of the others when you needed us."

"I've had a very difficult life, Tabby. I've seen and done things that would turn your hair white and age you considerably." She hugged him, put both her arms around him and held him tightly. "Tabby, you're going to make this big Marine cry if you keep being nice to me, and that's not anything to be proud of."

"I'll never tell." That little three-word sentence had him fighting harder than he'd had as a child to not let anyone see him cry. It meant so much to him that he leaned down to her and sobbed on her shoulder.

"I've never been this emotional before." She said it was because he'd never been allowed to be emotional before. "Christ, Tabby, you're going to make me a weak-assed man if I hang out with you and the others too much."

"Then stay with us forever, and I'll fight your battles for you when you need it. Any one of us will." He nodded, unable to speak around the lump in his throat and the melting of his heart. She pulled back and looked up at him. "Come on now. You get cleaned up, and we'll put your things in the limo. We'll have a lovely dinner, and then you'll go back home with us and meet your nieces and nephews. They're a hoot, and you'll love them too."

Before he knew it, Harlin was in the back of a limo with the other six. After Caleb had a long conversation with the realtor, Harlin found himself sitting in a nice restaurant with his family. Family. It had a really nice ring to it, and he might like to get used to having them around.

"I've bought the house for the amount you were asking. Next week, if you'd not mind, I'm going to have it torn down, and one put in its place. It'll be a rental that will be taken care of by my attorneys, and the money will go to the care of your mother. She might be a horrible person, but she's your mom, and that's the way she'll be taken care of." Harlin thanked him. "You're very welcome. We're family now, and family takes care of each other."

Yes, Harlin thought, he could really get used to this family thing. To have people supporting you like this wasn't anything that he wanted to make a habit of. He was, after all, a grown man, but for the time being, he wanted to be able to lean on them as much as he needed. It was a new concept for him. To have someone to lean on.

Chapter 6

Gracie had only been working in this restaurant for an hour when she figured out what was going on with the P&L report that was coming from the place. Now that she'd been here for ten days, she was ready to send her report off to Kylie, Caleb's attorney, to tell them what was going on. Gracie had been sending reports back nightly, but she wasn't going to be able to be here much longer without bashing some heads together. She even had a suggestion about who they should hire as the managing staff to take over for the prick that worked here now.

Mark's Steakhouse had not just an absent manager, but it also had spotty times when it was open. Mostly at breakfast time, no one would be here to cover the shift or even to open the doors. However, dinners were erratic as well. Arnold Becker, the general manager of the place, was a drinker. Gracie was positive that he had at least a dozen different bottles of something stashed in his office. So far, she'd counted fifteen in the walk-in cooler that were switched out daily for another full bottle.

Three times in the week and a half she'd been there, she'd had to wait until someone came in to let her in at five-thirty to start her dishwashing job. The manager had been scheduled to come in at five to open the place up on those three days.

Always the same server, Carlin Webber, came in to open up the restaurant on both the manager's and his days. Even coming in on his days off to do so. He also did the scheduling, ordering as well as making sure that shifts were covered for Becker when he was just too drunk or hung over to come in. Gracie knew just how Webber was feeling. With the exception of Billows just being lazy and not a drunk, it was the same situation.

Never once had Becker done more than show

up around noon or later, stagger to his office and slam the door. Then at dinner time, around six or seven, he would stagger out again and go home. Or to another bar. She didn't care after he left work.

Gracie had a feeling that he might well be taking money — another thing that Billows didn't do — to supplement his drinking. All their payroll checks went directly to their bank accounts, and she knew for a fact that Becker was married.

Elaine had been in once to see her husband. Gracie had been on break when she came in and had a good view of what the office looked like, where Becker was sprawled out on the floor and his wife kicking him a few times to wake him. She'd been demanding money. She had things to take care of, she'd told him. Gracie figured but wasn't positive that the money that Mrs. Becker needed was coming directly from the safe.

Daily, Webber would have to wait on some sales in the morning to be able to run to the bank and make change for the few customers that came in that early in the morning. Lunch was even worse for keeping enough money around to use the till, especially on a Fridays and Saturdays. That's when people would have larger bills to use from payday. Since she'd done the deposits and cash drawers at Devonshire, Gracie never had that issue. Thankfully.

"Miss Jefferies? There's a phone call for you." She tensed up, wondering if anything had happened to Martin, when she picked up the phone in the long kitchen. There was no privacy but in the office, and she hadn't been allowed in that place since she arrived. The call was from Tabby.

"I'm to tell you that Caleb is in the lobby, and I'm going to join him in a few minutes." Gracie told her that was nice. "Is the boss in? He so wants him not to be. Or drunk. I've really enjoyed the reports you send to Caleb. I bet that I can guess who is who by your notes."

"Yes, that'll be fine with me. I was about finished up with the book anyway." Tabby asked her if she'd found out everything so far. "It is. Very much so. I've been wondering what to do about all that stuff, so thank you for letting me know that you're going to be taking care of it."

"Slip out the back door, and after changing in the limo, join us. Caleb is as excited about this as I am.

Don't you think that it's working out well?" Gracie said that she was and would see her soon. "Thank you for this, Gracie. See you soon."

When the next half-empty tub of dishes was set on the counter, she said she was going to take a break. Slipping out the back door to find the limo right there waiting on her, she pulled off the nasty shit she'd been required to wear to work in and pulled on the jeans and shirt that had been brought for her. Getting out of the limo, she was thrilled beyond words to find Martin there waiting for her. After a quick kiss, they started to round the building to the front to go inside with Tabby and Caleb.

"Harlin is staying at the house that he likes from the ones that Caleb had purchased for us when we arrived. I'm not sure what Harlin's plans are, but I'm glad he's moving things along that far." She said that she was glad that he'd come home with them last night. "I am as well. Caleb is having the attorneys read over the books that Harlin's mother had written in. There are quite a few of them too. Caleb said he didn't think he was ready for whatever Howard did to kidnap and rape his mother. I'm not either, to be honest with you."

"I doubt that I'd be either." They were seated by Webber, who didn't even glance at her. She was sort of glad for that. Gracie didn't want any hard feelings when it came to firing Becker and then having him and his wife arrested. "Are the police on standby, Caleb?"

"Yes. Thank you for the heads up on that. I'm hoping that the next place you go won't have a lazy bastard working for me, and something like just terrible meals is all that's keeping people from going there." She told him good luck with that. "Yeah, I'm beginning to think that too."

Martin ordered for her so that the staff didn't hear her voice. After the order was taken and salads brought to them, she handed Caleb what she'd been able to find out when snooping around last night. Having a key to the place had helped her a great deal. But not with the office that Becket was sleeping in.

"I couldn't get into the office. He has not only a different lock on it that you were told about, but there are also three padlocks on it that have to be opened too. The cash drawer is left in the register every night, usually empty but for a couple of ones." She told him about the way they had to cash out sales the other night.

"Carlin Webber would be a great fit for running this place. He mostly is, anyway. However, you're going to have to fire the wait staff completely but for him. They're fucking lazy. The cooks are great. A little on the lazy side, too, but that's more, I think, from not having too many to cook for than they're not working. When the lunch crowd comes in, they work well together and get the meals out quickly."

"There will be a shutdown of the restaurant for about a month. Thank you for suggesting using that time to do some major updates. An auditor will be in starting tomorrow to go over the restaurant's receipts and deposits." She nodded at Caleb. "Are you all right doing this? I don't know why but I thought it would take you longer to get things figured out."

"Figuring out that Becker was a drunk was easy enough. Everything else sort of fell into place after I figured that out. The money being stolen was almost handed to me in that going on. The first time that Carlin came to the back room and asked if any of us had any money that he could use until he got to the bank was an eye-opener. It seemed to me then that everyone knew that the place was in trouble." Tabby asked if the staff was willing to help out. "Yes. They each looked like they'd brought in some cash just for that reason. Also, I don't want him to get into trouble for feeding them all, either. They're a good team, and Carlin is taking care of his staff better than anyone I've seen. Not only does he make sure that they're fed, but leftovers are put out for them to take home with them too. That right there is the only reason that they've not all walked out in the first place."

The police showed up just after the breakfast rush—even as small as it was—and closed the place down. It took them using a battering ram to get the office door open, and she got her first look at what was in the place. Christ, it was much worse than she thought.

There was nothing on the desk but a pillow and a thick foam mattress on it. The phone was an old one that looked like from the seventies that had places for putting people on hold and transfer. To whom, she hadn't any idea, but it was there to use.

There was a pillow in a plastic bag, and a sleeping bag was rolled up in a roll near the door. There were no filing cabinets in there, nothing to make it look like an office other than the desk that was being used as a bed. The safe, which was wide open, was empty of even bank bags. Nothing to do with any kind of running of a restaurant but more to do with a place for Becker to sleep. Also, they found several thousand dollars worth of alcohol and drugs in the room. Not even hidden away but in plastic medicine bottles and plastic bags all over the floor.

No sign of Becker or his wife, but it was still before noon at the restaurant. Sending three cruisers to Becker's home had the officers finding the two of them sleeping off whatever they'd been up to and money lying all over the house in stacks, apparently. Christ, this was going to cost the Becker's their lives in prison for what they'd found so far.

Gracie was asked questions by the police when it was discovered by just a simple glance at the bookwork that the place was missing well over fifty grand. The FBI was brought in as well. Caleb also answered questions as the owner of the place, and he was going to press charges against the Beckers as well as the working staff. Then she and Caleb, with Martin and Tabby, sat down with Carlin.

"I didn't do anything, Mr. Anderson, but try and make sure that the employees here were given a job. Payroll, I think, was only met because I'd found a way to send the hours to the company that does the checks for us." Caleb said that he'd figured that out. "Thank goodness. This could have been a good place, but since there wasn't much in the way of money to work with, I didn't have any idea how to make this place shine like it should have been doing all along."

"Would you like to have the chance of making this restaurant shine, Carlin? I'm willing to pay you a good salary with perks if you think you can bring some life into this place." Carlin asked him what that would entail. "I'm going to close the place down for a month. You'll be paid while this is going on and have the kitchen and all the other areas updated. I would think too that this would be a good time for the office to be enlarged for a safe that would be useful. You'd be able to hire anyone who would be able to pass a background check. All the people here, unless you say differently, will be terminated with unemployment starting tomorrow."

"No, sir. I'd not want to keep any of them

around. With exception of the dishwasher. She was a good joe and helped me out a few times when I needed it." Caleb introduced Carlin to Gracie. "I had no…well, don't you clean up nicely. You helped me on more than one occasion, Ms. Hamilton. There were times…well, I think you know that I was on the verge of not coming back to this place. I can't thank you enough for that."

"I knew you to be a good employee, Carlin. A trustworthy person too. I also want to tell you that Caleb is a man of his word. So long as you don't fuck him over, he'll make sure you have everything you need to make this restaurant run like a dream." Carlin asked her if she'd be around. "Not here, no, but I'll make sure you have my phone number if you need me. Even if it's just for me to tell you that you're doing a good job. I swear to you, you couldn't work for a better person. He's a prick at times, but I think that's just us."

Carlin laughed, and the rest of the table did as well. When Caleb told Carlin that he'd talk to him in a week, for him to enjoy being at home and resting up for a few days. Carlin had a couple of suggestions for the restaurant since it was going to be upgraded. One of the things that she thought was the best idea was to have a nice breakroom for the employees as well as a couple of lockers for them to put their things. Caleb agreed with him.

"Ready to head back home?" Gracie was so ready to go home that she nearly shook her hair loose from the rubber band she had holding her hair back. "I am as well. You will have to come out to the greenhouse with me. The water system is being put in right now and then the glass will be installed. I've never been so excited to start something as I am this. Harlin is going to help me too, which will be good for us both in getting to know each other."

The two of them talked all the way back to her hotel room. Once she was packed up and ready to go, Caleb and Tabby joined them. In less time than she thought it would have taken them on a public airline service, the four of them were headed home. She wanted to sleep in her own bed so badly.

~*~

Martin listened to the man that had installed the water lines. Also, he was showing him how to use the extra hoses and wiring to have an automatic watering system for the large planters that would be hanging from the front of the building when it was finished up.

"The furnace will be something that you can use year-round, but I don't see you having a need for it so much in the summer." Other than early spring, Martin asked him what they'd need the heat for in the winter months. "You might want to sell off some trees. There hasn't been a person selling real trees around here for a long time. When I was a kid, there used to be trees in this place that would rent you a tree for the holiday season. A person could come in and rent a tree that was balled up with their roots. Once the holiday was finished, they'd bring the tree back and decide if they wanted to rent it again next year or have it planted in their front yard. Lots of young couples would get it for their first Christmas together then plant it in their yard if they had themselves a plot of land to do that with."

"I love that idea. That would be a lot less in the landfill, too, don't you think?" The man nodded and continued explaining the system to him and Harlin. Harlin looked like a kid getting his first chemistry set and couldn't wait to play with it. "We'll be all right here, don't you think, Harlin?"

"Oh yes. It's been a dream of mine to have a way

to grow my plants since I was a child. We lived in the projects for a long time where you'd be lucky if you could get a dandelion to grow, much less a tomato." He had a strange smile on his face as he continued. "When I was sent away from home to the military school, we were required to spend some time in the gardens. Those gardens supplemented our meals a lot more than I think other kids realized. They were mostly city kids. Me too, but it was nice to be able to pick a fresh tomato and bite into it. Man, a little salt on it, and I'd be in heaven."

Sometimes Martin thought that Harlin was an old soul in a younger man's body. He had these old-fashioned sayings and idioms that would make him laugh because he'd not heard them since his grandparents had passed away. He was the calmest man that he'd ever met too. Nothing seemed to bother him. Martin asked him about that.

"I've lived about a million lives since I was born it felt like to me my whole life. My mother was insane and not willing to acknowledge that, as her child, I would need things that she should have provided. Having Howard there since my birth, that time had taught me how to be quiet and turn myself off when I was being beaten or worse." Martin told him how sorry he was about that. "Thank you, Martin. I know you mean it, but it wasn't your fault. Then, in military school, it was the perfect place for me. There were times when things had to be done, and the structure of all that made it easy for me to follow the rule. After graduating from there with honors, I slipped into the role of a servicemember easily. Even though things would be a major fuck up at times, there was still a regiment that I liked being a part of."

"I'm glad that you came back with us. I know that you don't know what you're plans are after all the dust is settled, but I do hope, no matter what you want to do, that you keep in touch with us." He said that he'd not decided yet, but he would, simply because he was enjoying having someone that he could depend on and talk to. "I'm glad for that. It's been good for us too. Caleb was just telling me on the way back from Tennessee that he was glad that his mom had done the hard work for him. He was very happy to have family around again."

The two of them looked through catalogs for

things that they could put in the greenhouse for autumn and Christmas. The idea of selling cut trees was appealing to them both. He was going to have to talk to Caleb about the land behind the greenhouse proper. There were so many fir like trees back there that he had to wonder if they were a part of the place before it had fallen apart.

Harlin was going to come to their house for dinner tonight. The grill that they'd ordered had arrived, and Gracie had it together in no time. He'd still be reading over the instructions on how to make part 'a' work into part 'b' but she seemed adept at reading them over and just putting it together. Martin was happy that at least one of them could change a tire if necessary.

Gracie came home about an hour after he and Harlin arrived. She had Yazzie, Joey and the kids with her, so they invited Caleb and Tabby to join them too. Martin thought it was wonderful not to have to worry about money. Not that he had a lot to worry with, but Caleb was paying Gracie well, and he was going to start, hopefully, making money at the greenhouse.

The kids were in the pool when Tabby arrived. Caleb was running behind, and since she didn't elaborate, he didn't ask. Martin enjoyed that too about having family around. If anyone needed help, it was right there for them to get too. They were all generous with their time and resources. Joey pulled him aside and was laughing about the information that he had concerning Billows.

"I've been talking to the officers at the jail where Billows is currently incarcerated. He's putting up a fuss about how he shouldn't be in trouble for having Gracie do all the work while he reaped in the money he was making. He is saying that it's all her fault for making it so easy for him to slack off and that Gracie should be in jail too." Martin laughed and asked what everyone was saying. "Mostly, they just roll their eyes at him, but a few of them have mentioned that had he been a good manager in the first place, Gracie wouldn't have had to step up."

"I bet that went over well, do you think?" Joey was still laughing. "You have to tell me. If this has you this tickled, I'm sure that I don't want to miss anything about this idiot."

"He still believes that Gracie is at fault, but he has it in his head that Caleb is such a sap that he's going to hire him back when the place is in better shape. He seems to think that he'll enjoy working for a brand new restaurant." Martin asked about the jail time. "Oh, that won't matter, he's telling them. Caleb won't even come looking again for another ten years or so, and he'll have things just the way that he wants them."

"I do wonder if there are any good restaurant managers out there. I know that there are. I bet that there are more than the ones like Billows and the other two that Gracie has found. I think she's doing an amazing job just being able to slip into the rooms where things are being cooked and served, then slip out like she wasn't even there." Joey agreed with him.

When Caleb arrived, he had gift bags with him. After he sat them around the dining room table, he joined them all out on the deck. This was his favorite part of his new home. The huge deck and the swimming pool. A hot tub was coming tomorrow for the area back here as well as some office equipment and supplies for Gracie to use. He was going to have his own office as well so that he could run the greenhouse from home when necessary. Picking up George, the youngest of Joey's children, Martin took him to the pool and let him splash around in the shallow end of the pool. He loved how the other children were very protective of their younger siblings and gladly made sure that they could see that he wasn't scaring the three year old. He thought that of all of Yazzie's and Joey's children, his favorite was Carol.

She could give you a look that made your skin move. She wasn't evil. No, she was a sweetheart when she wanted to be. But if you ever got out of line with one of the other kids, she would give you all the what-for a six year old could give an adult. Carol actually scared him a little at times. But he did love her. Martin loved all the kids.

He and Gracie had talked about having children on the way home last night. She was terrified of being a terrible mother. Martin had seen her around the other kids, and he was sure that she'd be perfect. She also told him that she'd like to adopt a couple of kids, too, if he thought that would be all right.

"I'd be happy to be a dad to anyone at this point in my life. Even a seventeen year old." They both laughed. "You tell me when you're ready to have children, and we'll work on that. Although I think that we should keep making sure that we don't get out of practice while you're waiting."

"It's doubtful to me that you'll ever get out of practice. How many times a day do we make love as it is now? Four or five. It would be more than that, I'm betting, if I didn't have to go to work all the time." He wiggled his brows at her. "You're goofy, Martin Hamilton. I love you to pieces, but you're off your rocker if you think that we, especially you need any more practice at making a baby."

Picking her up, he sat her on his lap when Yazzie took George to feed him his dinner. The kid was turning out to be a big boy, and Martin was looking forward to seeing him play football if that was his thing. Gracie leaned back on his chest as he dangled his legs in the warm water.

"I don't have to travel for the next couple of weeks. Carlin is going to be set up in another store, one that I've never heard of and shown how to be a manager and do things like scheduling and ordering. It's not one that Caleb owns, but he's good friends with the people who own it, and they're willing to help out." Martin didn't ask her how she felt about that. There was something bothering her, and he'd wait her out. "I'm going to need a car before too much longer. I've been walking anywhere I need to go. While I've full use of the limo, it seems silly to me to take it to the store when I want something to snack on. What do you think about going to the hospital with me to see the newborn that was left behind?"

"Right now is fine with me. Does anyone else know about it?" She said that Yazzie had told her earlier and that she and Joey decided that, for now, five was enough for them. "Christ, I should hope so. They're good kids, and I love them to pieces, but I'm not sure how they're doing it, especially with Yazzie being blind. I don't have any idea how she keeps track of all of them. But I'm betting that she'd tell you if you were to ask that it's because she loves them, and they love her."

"She'd be right too." She stood up and gave him a hand to help him stand. "If we leave now, we can be back in time for dinner. I've already spoken to the staff there, and since Caleb has vouched for us, we're able to take her right now."

"I was wondering what kind of baby we were

getting. Anything else I should know before she calls me daddy?" Gracie told him that she'd been told she was a perfect little girl. "Well, of course, she is. She's going to be a Hamilton, after all."

Telling no one but Joey and Yazzie where they were going, the two of them slipped into the limo and made their way to the hospital. The nursery staff was telling them what a pretty little thing she was while they waited on her to come from the nursery.

"Her mom was told that it was college being paid for or the child but not both. I know that it's done, but I can't believe that in this day and age that people are so set against having their children have little ones." Martin asked the nurse if there was trouble with the conception. "No. Not that I'm aware of. Just two twenty year old kids having a good time and a baby is a result of it. The young woman has her heart set on being a physician and needs the help of her parents. However, I don't think that after she's finished with college, she's going to have much to do with them. Also, she is aware that giving up the baby at this point in its life means that it'll have a better life than she could do for it and going to college."

"Do you think she'll come back for her?" The nurse, Danielle Bishop, said that once the paperwork was signed from the police that the child was left here after they'd been discharged, there was nothing she could do. "So the baby is considered abandoned."

"Yes. Once that happens, then they give up all rights to the child." Martin saw the little bassinet coming toward them and wanted to knock the nurse bringing the bed toward them out of the way so that he could see his daughter. As soon as he looked down at her red downy colored hair, he was in love.

"Oh, Martin, just look at her. She's perfect." He waited until Gracie picked her up before he sat down on the floor beside her. After stripping the little girl down to her diaper, they counted her fingers and toes twice before dressing her again. "Does she have a name yet?"

"No. she didn't name her. The birth certificate has the parents on it but nothing for the name. I was told to make sure that you two named her, and then we'll get the adoption paperwork filled out for the two of you. Also, since this is going to be an open adoption, you'll have all the medical information from both parents but without names. You'll have to get a court order to be able to find that information out."

They were headed home when they talked about names. Since she didn't want to name anyone after her side of the family and Martin didn't know anyone but his mom's first name, they had a middle name to contend with.

"Abigail. Without her, none of this would have come to pass." Martin loved the idea of naming their child after Caleb's mom. "We'll check with him first. Or do you think if he wants to name his own child that? "How about Anderson then. Shelby Anderson Hamilton."

Martin was beyond touched with the name. He was sure that his mom might have been happy. Perhaps not, but he didn't care. Martin was thrilled beyond words that his little family was growing.

Chapter 7

Raven stood up when her client, Mrs. Glenna Pastor, was called to hear her side of the trouble that her children were causing her. Stating Mrs. Pastor's name and Rayne's affiliation with her, the judge asked her what was going on.

"Mrs. Pastor has been in a nursing home for the last ten years, your honor. The state takes her social security checks each month as payment, as well as her pension from working for the state as a road crew when she was stronger. Her children, the four of them, are now requesting that she come live with them throughout the year, each of them taking her for three months at a time. As specified in the contract with the nursing home, if Mrs. Pastor is too much for the children, they'll no longer be able to return her to the nursing home. Ever." Judge Sheppard asked what the issue was. "Mrs. Pastor doesn't want to live with them. They treated her poorly when she was living with them before she was able to get into the nursing home. This is the fifth time that they've decided that they want her to come and live with them. Each time, she gets poor care from them and usually ends up in the hospital with bed sores as well as dehydration and malnutrition. According to Mrs. Pastor, they would lock her in her room all day and night and only check on her to see if she was still alive or not. She doesn't want to go through that again, your honor."

"And you have proof of this?" Asking to come to the dais, she handed the paperwork from the last five home trials for the family to the judge. "It says here that her meds were never picked up on time and that according to her advocate, you, I'm assuming, they were sold off instead of given to her."

"They'd not care a fig newton if was starving or not, sir." Mrs. Pastor, for being in her late eighties, was as sharp as a tack. Also, she didn't suffer fools all that well. That's why Rayne had requested to be her guardian, and that was what most of this trial was going to be for. Hopefully. "Why that oldest one of mine—I'm ashamed to admit this to anyone—but he'd punish me like I'm a child by taking my food from me when I didn't make it to the bathroom on time. Ungrateful bastards. The lot of them. How was I to make it to the bathroom when it's nowhere close to my room, and they have big locks on the doors. I tell you, they're ungrateful. The only person in the world that treats me with any kind of dignity is this young woman right here. She's been my rock since this nightmare began. Those kids of mine need to spend time with themselves and not be trying to take all my money for their own pleasures. Why, when I was living with my daughter, she bought her a new car and wouldn't even take me to the doctors in it for fear of me wetting myself in it. I might be old, but I do know when I have to potty, for crip's sake. Then when she decided that she'd gotten all she could from me, she tossed me in a nursing home and lost her car." Mrs. Pastor laughed. "Got her car repossessed, too, on account of her not getting my checks anymore. That's all they care about.

Getting my pension and social security checks to spend on crapola they don't need. Darned kids. If I had to do it over, I'd of not bothered with them. Ungrateful... well, I already said that, but I think it bears repeating. They're ungrateful."

The judge was trying hard not to laugh. If he knew anything about the elderly woman, he'd be careful about laughing at her. While she used a wheelchair to get around, she could get around better than most people in their sixties.

"Ms. Tanner, you've been taking care of Mrs. Pastor for how long now?" She told him the last ten years. "And you're an attorney for her as well, I can see here."

"Yes, sir. I was working for a firm when her case came across my desk. I'd already decided that being an attorney wasn't what I wanted in life and had given my two weeks. Mr. Palmer, of Palmer and Palmer, told me that if I took care that Mrs. Pastor was well represented, he'd pay me my usual salary so long as I worked for her through them. I took the job after one visit with Mrs. Pastor, meeting her family at the same time." He asked her if she was still an attorney. "I am your honor. I keep my license up so that if something comes up, I will be prepared to care for all her needs."

"Mrs. Pastor, other than your pension and Social Security, is there any other money that could be had from your estate?" She told him that she had insurance out the wahoo. Again, the judge laughed but coughed to cover it when she glared at him. "I'm assuming that you have a will made out as to what happens to your wahoo money?"

"Yes, sir. Missy here wouldn't do that for me. She said that if I wanted to do anything with that, I should get me an estate attorney so that no one could say that whatever was in it that she'd not had a thing to do with it. Wouldn't even let me tell her what it was going to say nor who the attorney was." The judge said that was brilliant of her. "Well, she is a brilliant girl. No cobwebs between her ears, that's for sure."

"Mrs. Pastor, you are a pleasure to speak to today. If you and Ms. Tanner could wait here while I—" The back doors to the courtroom were opened with a loud bang. Every person in the room that was armed put their hands on their weapons. Even her. "What is the meaning of this intrusion? Who are you?"

The six people that came into the courtroom were none other than the four children of Mrs. Pastor, as well as two spouses. Rayne didn't know who the wives belonged to, but she was willing to bet that it made very little difference at the moment. After explaining to the judge who they were and a general name for the bunch of them, the six of them continued to argue about who got to sit at the front table to get this 'shit over with' so they could start getting paid.

The gavel banged on the dais several times before the idiots looked anywhere near being finished arguing. It wasn't until Mrs. Pastor put her fingers into her mouth and let out a shrill whistle. Raven was prepared for it as she'd heard her do it before, but the judge and the others in the courtroom were shocked to silence. Everyone but her children.

"Sit down and shut up before I have the lot of you arrested for being born." The oldest, William, said she wasn't able to do anything and she'd best be keeping her mouth shut. "You come on over here, William Hunter, and I'll show you what I can do and not do. You were told to be here at nine. It's nearly noon. Why can't you take instructions well enough to be on time to someplace? Are you more addled than I thought you might be?"

"Why do they need to make things so early in the morning for anyway? I was sleeping. Then April Showers comes along and jerks me out of my nice bed like she's got some right to doing that." William, his mother, called all her children by their first and middle names, so the kids referred to themselves that way as well glared at her. "What is she doing here anyway? I thought that this was just going to be you and us getting you home with us. Don't you want that, Momma? To come and live with your children instead of sitting around on your duff all day with none of us around?"

"Actually, no, I don't want to live with any of you. Having you around when you were little was bad enough. I like it just where I am." William asked his momma if she'd put her up to saying that. "You know, I do have a brain, you dummy. I can and do speak for myself. She's here because she don't have to be borrowing brain cells to know what time to be somewhere when you've been told a dozen times when it starts. Now sit your bottoms down and don't make me have to come over there. I will beat your bottoms. I should have done it more when you were little, and I'd have me a better set of children. But I put that blame squarely on the head of your father. Spoiled you, he did. Thinking your grander than you really are. Now hush, before I have one of you go out and pick me a switch off that tree out front so I can beat some — though I'm thinking that it won't matter a hill of beans — some sense into your heads."

The judge left the room at some point, but the bailiff stood by the other Prestons while in the courtroom. Every time one of them started to get loud, he'd tell them to shut up, never taking his hand off his weapon. Raven and Mrs. Pastor spoke quietly at the other table.

"If he comes back with you having to go to your family's home, I'm going to apply for being your guardian like we discussed." Mrs. Pastor told her that she should just apply for it anyway, as her idiots weren't going to be giving up. "I don't want to rock the boat any more than we have to. Some of the paperwork that the judge has is about me doing that for you. We'll just have to wait and see, I guess."

"I guess." She looked over at her children, so

Raven did the same. They were arguing again about who was going to take their mommy first. "They're fools. I hope someone sees that before they kill me off. They will, too. If I die on my own, they're not going to be happy about nothing ever again. And they'll come after you on account of you being my friend."

"I'm not worried bout them, Mrs. Pastor. You just worry about what kind of things you're going to do to your room when you get back to the nursing home. I'm glad they found you a room bigger apartment than the one you have now. It'll be nice for you to be able to have a sewing room again, I'm thinking." She said that was exciting her the most. "Good. Once this is all settle, hopefully in your favor, you can go on sewing and enjoying life to the fullest. You and I will still have our weekly shopping and lunch, and your children will just be a fart in the wind as you're so fond of calling them."

"I should have kicked them in the head more. Might have made something click in that empty space they have up there." She looked over her shoulder to her children before smiling again. "That Betsy Ann, she's put on a few pounds since her divorce. She keeps eating like she is, and she'll be in a nursing home too. Darned kids."

Glenna, as she insisted Raven call her, didn't care at all for her offspring. She was forever telling her that she'd not wanted her husband, much less any kids of his, when they married. But since he'd asked her daddy before asking her, she didn't get the opportunity to turn him down. Her father had her married off to Mr. Gleason Pastor before she had her wedding dress picked out. Something that she regretted more than marrying Gleason was not having a pretty wedding like all her cousins did.

Raven wasn't stupid. Not by a long shot. She was really brilliant. Graduating at the top of her class from Harvard, she not only had a doctorate in law, but she also had a degree in social humanities. That was why she was able to take care of Glenna herself and not have someone doing it for the elderly woman.

After an hour, the judge sent someone out to say they'd rejoin the courtroom at two. They were told to go and get some lunch, and he'd have his verdict. While Glenna and she were leaving the courtroom, William was asking when they got to say anything.

Raven didn't hear the answer, figuring that they'd get their say when they returned. Or not. They'd already pissed a lot of people off today.

They settled at the dairy bar across the street from the courthouse. It was really busy, and they opted to sit under the large willow tree that had several tables and chairs around it. After getting their food and drinks, Raven looked around the small town that she'd grown up in and wondered at all the new additions. She was particularly happy with the greenhouse renovations.

"Momma, you're going to buy us some lunch. We all left the house without our wallets. Just give me what you have on you, and we'll make due." Glenna told her son, Donald James, that she didn't have her wallet either, that Raven had bought for her. "Then she'll buy for us too. Give me your credit card, girly, and I'll think about returning it to you. You've caused us a lot of trouble. I hope you know that."

"Really? Not that it matters to me one lick, but I'm not giving you my credit card, nor am I going to purchase you any lunch." He asked her why not. "I don't like you. None of you, as a matter of fact. So if you indeed forgot your wallets, which I don't believe for a second, then ask your wife. I can see that she has a nice handbag that looks stuffed with something. I'm not going to feed you shit. Get away from here before I call the cops on you."

"You got no reason to call anyone on us, Blackbird. You have a stupid name, too, by the way." A man wearing a suit and tie came and sat with her and Glenna. While she had no idea who he was, it looked to her like Donald did. "You already called them on us? Why? We haven't done a thing wrong to you yet."

"I know that, but it's the 'yet' that bothers me the most. Go away, Donald, before I have you arrested for being a dumbass." The man stood up, but he didn't say a word. Raven could see the gun at his side as well as the one that was just under the hem of his suit coat. "Donald, I wouldn't mess with this man if I were you. He's smart enough to shoot first and not ever ask questions of you later."

Donald walked away, mumbling under his breath about how he was being mistreated again and again. When the man was brought his food, Glenna asked him who he was. The smile on the man was contagious, and she smiled back at him.

"I'm Joey Phillips. My wife and I were out walking with the kids after their orientation at the school when she heard the arguing about lunch. She's going to be joining us soon." Glenna asked if he was a cop. "I work for the government when they need me, but yes, mostly, I work for the local police department. May I ask what is going on with the Pastor kids?"

Glenna explained how sorry she was about them being her children. She also gave Joey the run down on what was going on with them. A lovely woman and five of the most beautiful children sat down with them. The kids were each carrying a boxed up lunch, and one of the staff brought out one for the mother.

It surprised her to figure out that the woman was blind. Joey introduced her to them by telling her where they were seated. He also told them the names and ages of their children. Then he explained, as most would forget about, where her food was located on her plate by using a clock numbers.

"I've been blind since childhood. Sometimes I can fool most people into believing I'm sighted, but when we're out in public, so I don't wear most of what I'm eating, I like to know where things are on my plate."

The kids were so polite in helping the youngest child, George, to get a cup of ketchup on his plate to dip his dog in. "They're all ready for school this fall, and we came out to celebrate."

"I loved school when I was younger." She wiped mustard off of Madison's face when she bit into her hotdog too. "I've been meaning to go back to study something else for a while now. But Mrs. Pastor has been keeping me on my toes."

"Oh, go on with you. You know that we're having fun." Raven laughed and said that they were. "If I can stay put, I'm going to be a good deal happier than I am right now."

They talked until it was time for them to go back into the courtroom. Joey joined them inside, telling them that he'd feel better if they had more representation than they did now. She was actually glad for the extra pair of eyes. Whatever the judge said, it wasn't going to be a good thing for anyone, no matter how it went.

~*~

Gracie was bored out of her mind. When Joey came into her office, she begged him for something to do. Laughing, he told her that he might just have a job for her to do. After explaining about the courthouse and the judge putting things off until tomorrow, he wanted to find out as much information as he could about the Pastor family before the morning.

After showing her how to get into the deep system of looking people up, she sat there for an hour, asking him questions about what would constitute good intel. Once she had it down, he left her to go home to his family. They were still in a celebrating mood, and he wanted to enjoy it with them. She didn't blame them one bit.

Andi, as they were going to call their daughter, was a newborn and all the things that came with that. She slept most of the day and night and only woke long enough to want a clean diaper and food. Andi didn't interact with them that much now. She didn't smile much either, nor cry either, but Gracie was sure that she'd have plenty to smile about when she was older. It was the waiting that was driving her batty.

The names that she'd been given to look into were fun. On the surface, they looked like a normal bunch of people that wanted to have their mother, an elderly woman that had at one time been a road crew worker, live with them. But the more she dug into their lives, the more afraid she was for the woman. Joey was going to come over for dinner with his family and Ms. Parsons and her advocate, but she couldn't wait that long to tell him what she'd discovered. As soon as he answered the phone, she launched into the information she'd found.

"William and his wife spent sixteen months in prison for writing checks on someone else's account. His fathers. The account was overdrawn by several thousand dollars in just three weeks after he was killed. His death had been ruled a homicide, but there doesn't seem to be a resolution as to who might have killed him. Betsy Pastor has also been in jail as recently as two weeks ago. Her crime was poisoning the neighbor's cats and dogs." When he asked her how many she'd killed and how she'd been caught, she realized that she wasn't speaking to Joey but to Harlin. She told him she was sorry.

"Don't be. I'm happy to help with this as well." He asked her again how many deaths there were and how she'd been caught. Gracie told him. "She actually laid their dead bodies on the front steps of their homes?

Christ, that's just sick."

"You have no idea. When she'd been asked why she'd done it, her only explanation was that she didn't have any children. That's all she said, no matter how many times they asked her. That she didn't have any children. I would have locked her up had that been me, but I'm like that." Harlin laughed. "They're coming over for dinner tonight. You should join them. Mrs. Pastor is funny. Joey told me that her advocate is someone that he admires. She's taking on this family with no real need to do so. I'm not sure what he meant by that, but it might be fun to have someone new at the table."

"I think I'm going to pass on that tonight. I have several projects going on right now, and they need my attention. Maybe next time." She said that she'd come and get him if he didn't make an effort next time. "I thank you for that. I've become a recluse since I've been here. Not that I've not been before, but I'm steadily becoming more so while I'm working on the projects with your husband. This is going to be fun for us both, I think."

"Martin has been telling me about you guys'

progress nightly. I also found out, unless he's already told you, that the tree farm behind the greenhouse belongs to Caleb as well. He's going to go out and help you cut them when the time is right." Harlin said that was good to know. "All right, I'll let you go back to doing nothing. I'm going to be looking deeper into these people's lives for a bit longer. If you need any of us, you know how to get in touch with us, right?"

"I do, and I thank you for that." After hanging up the phone, Harlin called her back. "I'll tell Joey what you've found. He's been hanging around the greenhouse a bit today. I think he might enjoy knowing something is going right for a change."

After hanging up the second time, she got to work again. It was still early. Just after three, she wanted to have enough information for the family before they arrived. While she didn't know what they were having for dinner, she was glad that when she asked their new cook if they had plenty for more people, she was thrilled to death to cook for so many. She supposed after working in the army as a cook, just having her and Martin to cook for was sort of a letdown. But she was enjoying having someone there to cook for them.

It gave Gracie more time to play with Andi when she was awake.

By the time dinner was ready and guests were arriving, she had more dirt on the four Pastor children than she ever dreamed possible. Why they were out and about and not locked away in some kind of mental facility was beyond her. They were mean too. Not just to each other, but that was bad enough. They were mean to anyone that crossed their paths, especially to their mom.

Glenna Pastor had been abused by her husband from the day they married until his death. Her children each of them had sent her to the hospital several times a month when they'd been living with her. The house was a blood bath, the report said when Glenna had been found by a neighbor one day when she noticed that the front door to her home was open. After that, she'd been in a nursing home to recover. From there, she stayed because her children had taken the home and sold it off for the cash. Glenna literally had nowhere to go once she was able to live on her own again.

Then after that, they scattered to the winds, coming by to see her when they thought they could get her checks. As soon as it was established to them that since she was staying in a state funded nursing home, the only way that they could get her checks was to care for her themselves. That lasted about four months. And in that time, Glenna was hospitalized twelve times in that period for all sorts of complications due to not being cared for properly. Now they were at it again. Trying to get her to live with them while they took her checks and pension.

"Bastards." She picked up Andi when she started to fuss. "You won't treat mommy like that, will you? I hope not. Those people need to have their butts kicked from here until The ninth Sunday of the month. I think that's the way my grandma used to say it."

Joining the others in the living room after changing Andi, she was glad now that she'd printed extra copies of what she'd found. After explaining everything she'd been looking into, she was happy to see that Raven was impressed. That the things she'd found hadn't been on any records that she'd been able to unearth.

"It has a lot to do with me finding things because of Joey. He helped me get started." Glenna said she'd been embarrassed about what her children had done to her and hadn't mentioned it. "You should have. This might just be the ticket you need to keep them away from you from now on. I'm not saying that they'll give up. I have a feeling that they won't, but it will be helpful to the judge to see the pattern they've been using against you."

"To think that I did at one time love them. I know this is a harsh thing to say, but I've not loved them since they killed off their father. I knew that they did it to kill me off, but he wasn't in the car when it was hit by a hit-and-run car. He wanted to pick up the kids from the movies they had gone to, and I was glad for him to do it. They killed him. I just know it." Gracie didn't say anything. She'd been thinking the same thing. "I'd like for them to just go away and not return. That's what I'm hoping for as this goes on."

"We're working on it, Glenna, I promise you." Dinner wasn't about the trial or any of the things that Glenna's children had done in the name of robbing their mother. It was about fun and laughter and the babies. Even Andi stayed awake longer than usual to be talked to by Glenna. She was quickly becoming her best friend, Gracie thought.

Chapter 8

Martin came rising up out of bed, climaxing hard enough to make his brain feel like he'd eaten gallons of ice cream, and he had a brain freeze. Just as he was coming around, his body catching up to his mind, he felt Gracie down under the covers, and she was skillfully making his cock hard again with her lovely warm mouth.

Lying back on the pillows, he told her how much he loved waking up this way. As she fondled his balls, sliding her hand up and down his cock, he had to close his eyes against the need to have them roll to the back of his head, never to return.

"Christ, woman, the things you do to me." She

laved his cock up and down. Using the moistness from her mouth to let her play freely with his balls. Every time he thought for sure she was going to bring him to peak again, she'd adjust her mouth or body, and he'd be moaning out in great pain. "Gracie, you're going to hurt me."

She looked up at him from beneath the sheet and smiled at him. Never once stopping to tell him anything, just giving his cock a good bath with her tongue and mouth. Even his balls, being abused by her, wasn't anything that he wanted her to stop doing. Every inhale of his breath caught on her movements, and Martin was positive that he was going to die the happiest man on earth.

When he begged her to let him fuck her, she took her time moving up his body. A nip here, a small kiss there. When she was at his navel, she laved his opening over and over, making him about as dizzy as he'd ever been. Pulling her up to his mouth, he kissed her deeply, tasting himself on her mouth and felt his cock harden all the more. As soon as she took him into her pussy, he threw back, crying out with the best climax that he'd ever had in his life. To date, anyway.

Even as his body was settling back to earth, the only place he could figure he'd be all right, Gracie was doing things to his body that had his cock hurting and his heart pounding hard enough that he was sure everyone in the state could hear it. It was just too much.

His body, abused and well-loved, was just too much for him. Putting his hands beneath her arms, he jerked her up over him, rolling her to her back and slammed deep into her heat. Christ, it was overload at the highest degree. Coming again, Martin knew he was as dead a man as he'd ever seen before and felt his eyes roll to the back of his head so hard that he could swear that he heard them hit.

Waking up, he was alone in bed. The curtains were opened, but the sun streaming in didn't seem to bother him nearly as much as being by himself and cold. Rolling out of bed to the side, he had to sit there for several minutes before he knew that he'd be able to stand. His wife was nowhere to be found, but that was all right with him. If she had needed him to help her come, he was sure that, like a small child, he would have begged, sobbing, for her to just leave him alone. Perhaps forever.

Getting up and holding onto his bed, he half staggered and limped his way to the bathroom. Turning on the water had him winching. Then even getting under the stinging spray had him whimper. Martin was thoroughly ashamed of himself. A grown fucking man acting like he was on his last minutes of life. He thought for sure that he was dying.

As he started to get dressed, he was feeling better. It also helped that he'd taken a few pain relievers as well as a hotter shower than he'd ever taken before. Deciding that shoes were out of the question, for now, Martin slipped on a pair of gym shorts as well as a sloppy tee and headed down to the kitchen. He could hear voices in there of his wife and cook.

Forgetting her name, he kissed Gracie, asking her the name of their cook as he had to man-wrestle Andi from her. After telling him her name was Shelia Humphrey, she took the baby back and asked him how he was feeling.

"Not as chipper as you are, apparently." Gracie kissed him on the shoulder as she got up to get a bottle for Andi. Handing him both the baby again and her warm bottle, he watched her suck down her lunch like he felt — only she was hungry, and he was sore. "How did I get to sleep in so late?"

"I couldn't wake you. For a while there, I thought you'd died in your sleep." They both laughed, but his was forced. Because Martin really had felt that way at one time last night. "But I'm not upset. I got to spend some time with Andi and Shelia. She was telling me about being a cook for the Army Corps when she was much younger. Then got recalled into service when her family moved away."

"I bet that was a huge cutting back on food." It was then that he remembered she was Scottish. He might well have to read up on her speech while she was here. Some of her wording was hard for him to understand. Then she set a plate of food in front of him. "Oh, my. If I wasn't already married, Shelia, I might take you on as my wife."

There was bacon and eggs, sausage, the link kind that he loved, fried potatoes as well as beans. He wasn't sure what the little brown patties were, but once biting into them, he was moaning in delight.

Martin set to work after lunch. It wasn't until he answered his phone that he realized that he was feeling pretty good. Getting up to find out what was going on for dinner for Gracie as she was still helping Joey, he was glad that they were having dinner alone tonight and were grilling out. He was thrilled, too, that Shelia told him she was grilling extras of the meat so that they could lunch on them while she was off the next day.

He was literally rubbing his hands together as he got back to work. Tomorrow was going to be an epic day. He hadn't any idea why but he was looking forward to being on some kind of normalcy. Whatever the hell that meant to him and his new family. Going upstairs to get his daughter, he was glad he was just in time to feed her the next bottle and then rock her to sleep.

Before You Go...

HELP AN AUTHOR

write a review

THANK YOU!

Share your voice and help guide other readers to these wonderful books. Even if it's only a line or two, your reviews help readers discover the author's books so they can continue creating stories that you'll love. Log in to your favorite retailer and leave a review. Thank you.

AWARD WINNING, BESTSELLING AUTHOR

Kathi Barton, a winner of the Pinnacle Book Achievement Award and a best-selling author on Amazon and All Romance books, lives in Nashport, Ohio, with her husband, Paul. When not creating new worlds and romance, Kathi and her husband enjoy camping and going to auctions. She can also be seen at county fairs with her husband, an artist and potter.

Her muse, a cross between Jimmy Stewart and Hugh Jackman, brings her stories to life for her readers in a way that has them coming back time and again for more. Her favorite genre is paranormal romance, with a great deal of spice. You can visit Kathi online and drop her an email if you'd like. She loves hearing from her fans. aaronskiss@gmail.com.

Follow Kathi on her blog: http://kathisbartonauthor.blogspot.com/

www.ingramcontent.com/pod-product-compliance
Lightning Source LLC
Chambersburg PA
CBHW032213190626
46810CB00019B/2918